Lady Margery's Intrigues

Also by Marion Chesney
in Large Print:

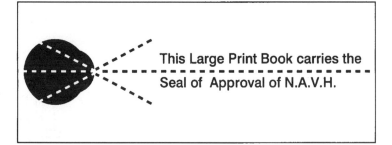

This Large Print Book carries the
Seal of Approval of N.A.V.H.

Lady Margery's Intrigues

Marion Chesney

Thorndike Press • Waterville, Maine

Copyright © 1980 Marion Chesney

Published in 2002 by arrangement with
Lowenstein Associates, Inc.

Thorndike Press Large Print Core Series.

The tree indicium is a trademark of Thorndike Press.

The text of this Large Print edition is unabridged.
Other aspects of the book may vary from the original edition.

Set in 16 pt. Plantin by Minnie B. Raven.

Printed in the United States on permanent paper.

Library of Congress Cataloging-in-Publication Data

Chesney, Marion.
    Lady Margery's intrigues / Marion Chesney.
      p. cm.
    ISBN 0-7838-9614-X (lg. print : hc : alk. paper)
    1. Large type books.   I. Title.
PR6053.H4535 L34 2002
  823′.914—dc21   2001051443

Lady Margery's Intrigues

Chapter One

"Only think, dear Amelia," said Lady Margery Quennell, looking around the glittering throng which graced Almack's Assembly Rooms. "After tonight, I will never have to endure another Wednesday night like this again."

Lady Margery was seated next to her aunt, Lady Amelia Carroll, on that uncomfortable piece of furniture known as a rout chair, in the shadow of one of the pillars which supported the musicians' gallery.

She raised her chicken-skin fan to her face to cover a yawn. "I told Papa it was no good sending me to London for season after season. I shall never 'take,' you know. And all this bores me so dreadfully."

Lady Amelia gave her comfortable laugh. "Only think, dear Margery," she whispered, "of all the young debutantes who cry and sob because they cannot enter the portals of Almack's. Henry Luttrell wrote a vastly amusing poem about it. He said:

'All on that magic List depends;
Fame, fortune, fashion, lovers, friends;

'Tis that which gratifies or vexes
All ranks, all ages, and both sexes.
If once to Almack's you belong,
Like monarchs you can do no wrong;
But banished thence on Wednesday night,
By Jove, you can do nothing right.' "

Lady Margery gave a reluctant laugh. "Well, I *am* here, and still I can do nothing right!"

A ball and a supper were given at Almack's once a week during the season; voucher-invitations were issued by the despotic partronesses, and girls new to the fashionable world wept and moaned if they were not on the list.

Lady Margery was aged twenty-three and had graced the rows of wallflowers for many a season, her choleric father, the Earl of Chelmswood, refusing to believe that his daughter was not a diamond of the first water.

She had just extracted a promise from him that never again should she have to waste money — which by rights should go to the maintenance of her home and estates — on the simply awful expense of a season.

"Won't you miss it all a little bit?" queried her aunt curiously.

Lady Margery let her eyes roam over the ballroom. "Not in the slightest," she whispered back. "Now if I were a gentleman, 'twould be a different matter. I could join the perpetual bachelors and have a marvelous time. Here come the top four prizes of the marriage mart."

Four gentlemen were just entering the ballroom — Viscount Swanley, a fair and willowy youth; the Honorable Toby Sanderson, a bluff country squire; Mr. Freddie Jamieson, handsome in a dark way but never quite drunk and never quite sober; and the Marquess of Edgecombe.

It was the last who made Lady Margery's pulses race although she knew the marquess to have the reputation of a hardened flirt. He was tall, with a languid grace which belied his athletic body. He wore his thick tawny hair unpowdered and longer than the current fashion dictated. He had a strong, very white, high-nosed, arrogant, masculine face. His eyes were of a startlingly vivid blue but were often veiled by heavy drooping lids and thick black lashes. His handsome face was marred by a perpetual air of boredom. Lady Margery had a sudden longing to see him smile.

The voice of her aunt broke into her thoughts. "There's Edgecombe," whispered Lady Amelia, waving her long ostrich-feather fan under Margery's nose. "He is reported to be paying court to little Miss Clarence — the latest belle, you know." Her fan tickled Margery's nose and Margery burst out in an awful sneeze and then gave her infectious laugh.

"Take that . . . that . . . *thing* away from under my nose, Amelia. I declare it's seen almost as many seasons as I."

At that moment, the marquess looked across the room and caught a glimpse of Lady Margery's face, animated with laughter. He found himself wondering who she was and turned to his friend, Freddie Jamieson.

"Freddie! Who is that girl over there under the musicians' gallery? The one seated next to that plump lady?"

Freddie tried to focus his bleary eyes and failed. He took out his quizzing glass and held it so far in front of him that the marquess thought, for one awful minute, he was going to fall over.

"Oh, that!" he said finally. "That's Lady Margery Quennell. Surely you have heard about her. Dreadful old father of hers drags her up to London, season after season, hoping someone will marry her. Poor girl! You've only to look at her to see why they won't. 'Course, the family's got precious little money either."

"She has a lovely smile," said the marquess, studying the interesting Lady Margery for the first time.

He saw a very small girl — she must have been only about five feet tall — dressed in an unfashionable gown of a hideous shade of puce. She had a neat figure and an attractive pair of gray eyes, but she had wispy, sandy hair and a thin white face.

It was not that she was precisely unattractive, he decided. It was simply that the girl positively radiated boredom. He had a sudden impulse to discover what the plain Lady Margery would look like when she was animated.

"He's coming this way," hissed Lady Amelia.

"Who? What?" demanded Lady Margery, whose mind had been busy with the repairs to her home — so busy that she had completely forgotten that she was at Almack's.

"The Marquess of Edgecombe!" muttered Amelia. "Smile!"

But Lady Margery was looking up into the handsome face of the marquess with all the enthusiasm with which the hare watches the approach of the weasel.

Then the marquess was bowing before her, his hand on his heart, and begging Aunt Amelia's permission to lead Margery into the waltz. She stood up. She dropped her fan. He bent to pick it up at the same time as she did and they banged their heads together. Lady Margery blushed and apologized. He held out his arms to lead her into the steps of the waltz and, to his horror, she collapsed headlong into them. Lady Margery had been sitting against the wall for so long that her foot had gone to sleep. Again she blushed and apologized, and the marquess cursed himself for being such a fool as to patronize plain wallflowers.

It was then that Lady Margery found her courage. To dance with the Marquess of Edgecombe was the same as dancing with Mr. Brummell — it was one of the highest social accolades. And Lady Margery was feminine and human enough to crave for just a little social success on her last night.

The marquess was thankful for small mercies. The small lady in his arms danced divinely, although so far he had only managed to look down on the top of her head.

She suddenly raised her eyes to his and smiled. Really, the little thing was quite fetching when she was animated! He plunged into conversation.

"Are you enjoying your season, Lady Margery?"

"Yes," she replied dutifully, and then added truthfully, "At least I *am* enjoying it *now*. I mean I am enjoying the fact that this is my last season, and after tonight I may never have to endure a ball or rout or breakfast or turtle dinner ever again."

The blue eyes mocked her. "You disappoint me, Lady Margery. I had hoped you were enjoying yourself *now* because you were dancing with me."

"Oh, I *am*," said Margery. "It is such social

prestige to be seen dancing with the Marquess of Edgecombe that I am sure I am the envy of every other lady."

"And *that* is the only reason you are enjoying your dance? Not because you are in my arms?"

"You must not flirt with me, my lord," said Margery gently. "I am not practiced in the art, you see."

"I could teach you," said the marquess lightly, wondering why he was behaving so badly.

"I am unteachable," said Margery sadly. "This is my third season, you know. My father refuses to admit that I will not 'take,' so he gives me one year of peace in the country and then insists on putting me through the mill again. I have become quite fond of my little chair over there, and perhaps when I am dead they will put a little placque on it saying, 'Lady Margery Quennell sat here. And sat. And sat.' "

"Had I noticed you before, Lady Margery," he said, executing a neat pirouette, "you would not have been left sitting."

"How very kind of you to say so, especially since you only pay court to beauties."

"And I still do," he said, smiling down at her in such a way that she felt a wrench at her heart. She began to feel quite breathless and was glad when the dance came to an end.

"Allow me to take you in to supper," said the marquess, surprising himself and Lady Margery. "I have dined already, and the food is quite dreadful here, but then I shall have a little more time in your company."

She put her head on one side rather like an inquisitive kitten and surveyed her tall escort. "Now, you *are* being kind," she said. "And you did not strike me as being a particularly kind man."

"How can you tell what people are like from just looking at them?" he asked, amused, as he escorted her to the supper room and surveyed the array of curling sandwiches and unexciting cakes.

"I have ample time to study people, you know, since I 'sit out' so much at balls and parties."

"Let us test your powers of deduction while we pretend to eat. What do you think of my friend Viscount Swanley, for example?"

Again Margery tilted her head to one side. "Let me see, Viscount Swanley — Lord Peregrine. Yes, I have noticed him. I would say he was a pleasant young man, good company, not much of a sportsman, and probably writes poetry in secret."

"Now that is too good," laughed the marquess. "Someone must have told you about the poetry although it is Perry's carefully guarded secret. Now what about Toby Sanderson?"

14

"Oh, very much the country squire and sportsman. Gambles too much and would bet on anything. Terrified of women which is why he is still a bachelor. Pays court only to beauties, knowing he has no hope of marrying one."

"Bravo! And what about me, my cynic?"

Everyone was furtively watching them. Lady Margery was enjoying the very heady novelty of knowing that she was a success.

"A bit of the poet, a bit of the sportsman, a bit of the lover, and very much the cynic. Never married because . . . because he was very disappointed in love at an early age and has privately despised women ever since."

"Lady Margery!"

But Margery was carried away and had almost forgotten who she was talking to. "He will probably marry eventually, but only to secure an heir, and he will marry the Beauty of the Season as a matter of form. He —"

"Allow me to escort you back to your aunt."

The marquess's voice was like ice and his eyes were blazing with anger. Lady Margery stared at him in dismay. The animation slowly left her face and the sparkle went from her eyes. A plain and colorless Lady Margery was escorted back into the ballroom by the marquess, who gave her a slight bow and left.

Margery longed to tell her aunt of her

wretched social error, but she was not to be allowed an opportunity until much later. Where the marquess led, the fashionable world followed, and everyone wanted to see what the marquess had found so amusing and fascinating in plain Lady Margery. Her dance card was quickly filled. She was a great success. Determined to show the haughty marquess that he had not crushed her, she sparkled and flirted and laughed as never before, while Lady Amelia looked on in amazement.

"What a marvelous evening!" exclaimed Lady Amelia finally, as they stood on the steps of Almack's and waited for their carriage.

It was a beautiful spring night, clear and warm, with the scent of limes from the park mingling with the less attractive smell of whale oil from the parish lamps.

"And how marvelous of the Marquess of Edgecombe to bring you into fashion. What a pity you shall not have an opportunity to see him again."

"A pity!" snapped Margery, near to tears. "It's a blessing!"

How could she tell her aunt that, until now, she had been able to endure the boredom of the social round because she was heart-free?

She was furious with the handsome marquess for having made her heart beat faster, and furious at herself for having childishly annoyed him and driven him away.

Her stockings were coming down and her shawl had become entangled in the beads of her necklace.

She felt dowdier and plainer than she had ever done in her life before.

She never wanted to see the Marquess of Edgecombe again!

Chapter Two

Chelmswood was rarely to be found in any guides to homes of the British aristocracy. There was nothing about it at first sight to excite the public interest.

It was an old Tudor pile built of rose-red brick with mullioned windows and tall ornate chimneys, built into a fold of the Sussex downs. Many considered it a very unpretentious home for the Earl of Chelmswood, and the earl himself had damned it as a "drafty, poky place" but it was Lady Margery's only love.

She loved the low-paneled rooms with their great, gaping fireplaces, and the long, winding galleries and corridors so full of surprising steps up and steps down to trip the unwary. She loved the sprawling lawns with their huge beech trees and the heady scents of the formal rose garden, which was the pride and joy of a crusty Scottish gardener named McKinnon.

A week had gone past since the end of the London season, and Lady Margery, looking round the pleasant morning room with its homely clutter of books and sewing, felt as if she had never been away. Sometimes the handsome face of the marquess rose up before her eyes to mock her with a feeling of opportunities lost, but she quickly shrugged it away.

She had not seen her father since her return. Lady Amelia had informed her sourly that her papa was "junketing in London" and, last heard, had stated that he had plans for moving to Brighton with the Prince Regent's court — "though where your papa gets the money to run with Prinny's set, I'll never know," said Lady Amelia.

Margery looked over at her aunt with affection. Lady Amelia Carroll was a buxom matron in her fifties, widowed at an early age and now long accustomed to her single state. She enjoyed her unpaid post as friend and companion to Lady Margery. Both women had much the same tastes, enjoying the simple life of the country with its round of genteel calls on the local gentry and its unpretentious amusements.

Lady Amelia could not help sighing a little as she looked across at her younger companion. Lady Margery, she felt, would have had much more success with the gentlemen if they could have seen her in her home setting. The country air had brought the roses back to Margery's white cheeks, and she wore her sandy hair brushed and shining in a simple style. The plain blue muslin high-waisted gown was of Margery's own making and was much more attractive than her fashionable wardrobe, which had been chosen for her by one of her father's many lady friends.

But no gentleman was likely to view the country edition of Lady Margery. Their few neighbors were mostly elderly people or couples with daughters of their own to push onto the marriage mart.

The clatter of wheels in the carriageway announced the arrival of a visitor.

"Now who can that be?" murmured Margery placidly, not bothering to rise. "Perhaps it is Mrs. Skeffington from the rectory with that recipe for tansy pudding."

She heard the slow, laborious steps of Chuffley, their ancient butler, crossing the vast acreage of the hall to greet the arrivals. And the rumble of a familiar masculine voice.

"Papa!" cried Margery, throwing down her sewing and rushing to the door of the morning room, closely followed by Lady Amelia.

Both women stopped and looked across the gloomy expanse of the hall in surprise. The tenth Earl of Chelmswood stood at the entrance with a slightly sheepish smile on the ruin of his once handsome face. And clinging to his arm was a vision of loveliness. Butterblond curls peeped out from beneath a dashing poke bonnet, and the finest Indian muslin clung to an exquisite form.

"James!" Lady Amelia's voice was like ice. "We are accustomed to your escapades, but to bring one of your ladybirds —"

"Damn you, you long-nosed old harridan," roared the earl. "This is my wife!"

The earl and his new wife had retired to their quarters to change for dinner, and Lady Margery and Lady Amelia were left alone with their shock.

"How could he?" demanded Margery, her voice trembling with tears. "She cannot be a day over nineteen. To have a step-mama younger than oneself! And where did he find her? I declare, I was so shocked that I did not pay too much attention."

"Oh, she's good enough family," said Lady Amelia wearily. "Her name is, or was, Desdemona Bryce of the Bryces of Surrey. They're a poor family but gentry for all that. Your papa broke his axle on the road there and dropped in at their place for the night several months ago. He has evidently been courting her ever since but keeping the whole affair prodigious dark. Frightened we would put a spoke in his wheel, he said. And her family is no better. They consented to a havey-cavey wedding at their village church. No one was there but *her* family. I gather she has an exaggerated idea of your dear papa's wealth."

"So I gathered," said Margery grimly. She

ruthlessly mimicked Desdemona's die-away voice. " 'Oh, what a dirty old place, Jimmy. Not at all what I expected.' "

"Desdemona!" said Lady Amelia. "What a name! Mayhap he'll strangle her."

"Mayhap I will," said Margery, beginning to giggle. "Perhaps we are being too severe on the girl. I suppose I am to teach her the running of the house."

But when the vision that was the new countess joined them in the drawing room before dinner, it soon became evident that she had no intention of bothering her head over household affairs.

"I am sure you do it all so well, dear Margery," she said languidly. "After all, what else do you have to do? Jimmy tells me he has paid for season after season but nothing happened."

"No," said Margery baldly.

"Such a waste of poor Jimmy's money," said Desdemona.

She floated off into the dining room on the earl's arm before Margery could think of an answer.

Margery was proud of the fact that they kept a good table despite their straitened circumstances. Mulligatawny and turtle soups were followed by a salmon and a large turbot surrounded by smelts. This was in turn followed by a magnificent saddle of mutton, with a tongue, a ham, and two roast fowls.

"Such plain, simple country fare," sighed Desdemona. "The flavor is a trifle odd."

"It is perhaps because you eat our simple country fare so fashionably," said Margery dryly.

It was the custom to make a selection of the good things on the table and then attempt to place a portion of each in your mouth at the same time. Desdemona's plate, for example, contained a slice of fowl, a piece of stuffing, a sausage, a slice of tongue, cauliflower, and potatoes, and she had somehow managed to arrange a piece of each on her fork. As Gronow was to say in his *Recollections*, "It appeared to me that we used to do all our compound cookery between our jaws."

Margery could not decide whether Desdemona was being deliberately malicious or if she was simply stupid.

Desdemona was so surprised that her Jimmy had such an *old* daughter. They had not yet been on their honeymoon, she explained, blushing prettily. Jimmy was going to take her to Paris now that that monster was safely in Elba. She was simply *dying* for some Parisian dresses.

A faint summer breeze blew in from the open windows and sent the candle flames streaming. The wavering light danced on Margery's diamond-and-ruby necklace and it flashed and burned like fire.

Desdemona clapped her hands. "Ooooh! What a gorgeous necklace. Can I have it, Jimmy?"

"No, you can't," said the earl, rousing himself from a torpor induced by infatuation and wine. "Margery's mother left that to her. It's part of her dowry."

"But she'll never get married," said Desdemona, all pretty surprise. "And I want it."

The earl was not a man much used to having his will crossed. He promptly forgot his infatuation in a burst of his old choleric temper. "Damme," he said testily, "I've said 'no' and I mean *no*."

A wisp of fine lace appeared in Desdemona's hand as if produced by magic. "You're howwid to me, Jimmy," she sobbed. "Jimmy said he would get his baby anything she wanted."

The earl flushed the color of his wine and looked hunted. "Yes, yes, m'dear," he said hurriedly. "Dry your eyes now. We'll talk about it later."

"I want to talk about it *now*." Desdemona's voice had become increasingly shrill, and a firm L-shaped line had appeared along her jaw.

Margery and her aunt writhed in embarrassment. Never had either of them been subjected to such a vulgar scene, and never had either of them been so totally powerless to do anything about it. Desdemona was the new countess. This was now her home and she could do and say as she pleased.

"Drink your wine," said the earl desperately.

"Shan't!" screamed Desdemona. "I want to know, now! Now! *Now! Now!*" She was beginning to turn an alarming bluish shade and her breath was coming out in short bursts.

To Margery's horror, her father looked furtively at her and mumbled, "I say, Margie, y'don't suppose . . ."

"No," said Margery coldly. "It is the only valuable thing I possess and I intend to keep it."

"Buy you another," said her papa sulkily.

Margery looked at him in surprise. "You couldn't possibly afford to buy me another!"

Desdemona paused in mid-gulp and looked at the earl, her pretty eyes narrowing into slits. "You've got money, lots and lots of money, you know you have, Jimmy. Tell her!"

"There, there," said the earl, running a finger along the inside of his cravat. "Very rude to talk about money at table. Tell you after, what!"

He winked at his bride, who suddenly smiled back. Desdemona thought she had solved the problem. Naturally he did not want that dreadful daughter of his to know just how much he had.

Desdemona set herself to please. She told a

host of *on-dits* which Margery recognized as the gossip belonging to the season before last. The earl laughed at all the old stories as if he had never heard them before.

He was a large, beefy, jovial man who had once dazzled the salons of eighteenth-century London with his manly graces. Now in his middle fifties, he showed all the marks of an indulgent life of long hours of drinking and gambling. Margery's mother had died giving birth to her, and since then there had been no one to curb the earl's excesses. His new bride seemed to be in a fair way to encouraging them!

When Desdemona was in good humor, it was all too easy to see what had fascinated the earl, apart from her extreme youth. She was as pretty and dainty as a Dresden figurine, and had her family had enough money to launch her on a London season, they would not have looked twice at a middle-aged earl.

By the time dinner was finished, Margery felt she had been put through a wringer. Any remarks Desdemona addressed to her seemed to be made to the necklace that flashed and burned on Margery's bosom. Margery was beginning to see her home as it appeared in the eyes of this supercilious newcomer. For the first time she noticed the bare patches in the rugs and the worn upholstery on the chairs. The ceilings, which were blackened in the winters by gusts of smoke from the great fires, were badly in need of painting. She prayed silently that Papa would remove his bride to Paris as soon as possible.

She had not long to wait. It appeared the bridal couple were to depart on the following morning. Desdemona deposited an icy peck on her cheek before climbing into the great traveling carriage and leaving the earl alone to have a word with his daughter.

"You know, Margie," said the earl, shuffling his feet in the pebbles of the drive. "No one's denying you ain't a good housekeeper. But a man wants something more in life than just that. Seems to me you could do with a bit of training from a girl like Desdemona. She'd soon catch you a man, heh!"

Margery took a deep breath. "Your wife has been extremely unkind to me, Papa. She has made a great many cutting remarks, and I am surprised to hear you taking her part. The one thing you have never suffered before is ill-bred manners under your own roof."

"Hoity-toity, miss. You're just jealous," said the earl infuriatingly. "You'll get over it."

He gave his fulminating daughter a hearty slap on the back and plunged into the carriage. As the carriage lumbered off, Margery heard Desdemona titter, "What a dragon of a daughter, dear Jimmy! More like a mother-in-law," and heard his hearty laugh in reply.

Summer mellowed into autumn and still the earl showed no signs of returning home, leaving his daughter to cope with one financial blow after another. The first bad news was that the earl had sold his estate in Yorkshire for a considerable sum and had taken up permanent residence in an elaborate mansion in Grosvenor Square. News of the earl and his new countess's excesses filtered down even to the quiet backwater of Chelmswood.

Margery and Lady Amelia could only be thankful for small mercies. They had been left alone to pursue the quiet tenor of their country days unmarred by the demanding presence of the new countess, whose daring Parisian wardrobe and magnificent jewels were said to be the talk of London.

As the first snow began to fall, the earl's man of business, Mr. Harold Jessieman, arrived unexpectedly from London, demanding to see Lady Margery.

He could hardly wait for the elderly butler to take away his muffler and greatcoat before he burst into speech.

"My dear Lady Margery, I trust you are not one of those young ladies who are prone to fainting fits?" was his unauspicious opening.

"No," said Lady Margery. "Please tell me your news."

The little businessman straightened his wig

with chalky-white fingers and looked at her anxiously. "Perhaps it would be wise to call Lady Amelia . . ."

"My father!" gasped Lady Margery. "Speak up, man, for heaven's sake, or I *will* have an attack of the vapors."

"There is nothing physically wrong with your father," said Mr. Jessieman. "I almost wish that there were."

"Come now," said Lady Margery in what she hoped were bracing tones. "Let me fetch you some mulled wine to warm you. If father is well, there can be little wrong."

"I am not in the habit of making a journey in the middle of winter to discuss trivia," said Mr. Jessieman sharply. "The long and the short of it is that your father has squandered his inheritance at the gaming tables of St. James's in order to support his wife in a style of living to which she has become all too rapidly accustomed. I informed him that he must retire to the country and retrench. He simply laughed in that guilty way of his and told me not to be such an old stick and to find a buyer for Chelmswood!"

Lady Margery stood very still. The wind sighed gently through the great trees outside and the powdery snow whispered against the windows. She looked with wide eyes around the cozy, shabby room.

"Sell!"

"I appealed to him," went on Mr. Jessieman, looking at her nervously. She had turned as white as the snow drifting gently outside. "I reminded him that Chelmswood had been in his family for generations, and for a minute he seemed to be moved. Then Lady Desdemona came into the room. She immediately demanded to know what we were talking about, and the earl told her. She simply laughed in my face. Laughed! Said that 'her Jimmy' would be better off without that great barn of a place.

"I reminded her that it was *your* home that was being sold from under you."

"And what did she say to that?" asked Margery faintly.

"My lady suggested that Lady Amelia should find employment as a paid companion and that you, my lady, should go to London and become *her* companion. I assure you, Lady Margery, at this point your good father did try to protest, but she . . . she . . ."

"Go on!"

"The countess sat down on your father's knee — right in front of me — and wound her arms round his neck and persuaded him that it was all for the best and that she would find you a suitable husband."

"To which my father answered?"

"To which your father answered . . ." Here Mr. Jessieman hesitated and eyed his young hostess nervously. He then seemed to gather courage. "To which he answered," said Mr.

30

Jessieman, " 'My clever little puss, I never thought of that. Margery will be delighted.' "

Margery looked out of the windows at the falling snow. It was all too dreadful and all too true. She could just picture Desdemona cajoling her naïve father and persuading him that Margery would be ecstatic over the idea of living as a companion under the cat's-paw of Desdemona.

There was nothing Margery could do or say. She noticed that Mr. Jessieman was looking fatigued after his journey and rang the bell so that the butler could show him to his rooms.

Left to herself, she paced the room nervously and wondered what on earth or how on earth she was to tell Lady Amelia. The wind moaned in the chimney like a cry from her heart.

Never in her life before had she felt so weak or so feminine. She suddenly longed for a pair of strong masculine arms to comfort her and for a strong masculine shoulder to cry on. She thought fleetingly of the Marquess of Edgecombe and then laughed at her fancy. The elegant marquess was the type of man to complain that she was ruining his jacket if she ever cried on *his* shoulder.

Lady Amelia bustled into the room, bringing with her a gust of cold air from the hall that sent the worn tapestries on the walls shaking.

"Chuffley tells me Mr. Jessieman is here. No bad news of the earl, I trust?" asked Lady Amelia, studying her young friend's strained face.

In a halting voice, Margery told Lady Amelia of their fate as planned for them by the Countess of Chelmswood.

Lady Amelia clutched onto a chair back for support. The chair skidded on the floor and crashed into a music box, which threw up its lid and sent its silly tinkling Georgian love songs through the shadowy room. Lady Amelia had been rescued from a life of genteel poverty by the haphazard generosity of the earl. She was all too well aware of the drudgery of a paid companion's life.

Her plump hands fluttered helplessly to her face. "Is there anything we can do? Oh, my dear, if only you had made an advantageous marriage . . . Oh, forgive me . . ."

"I shall."

Lady Margery had spoken the two words so quietly that Lady Amelia wondered if she had imagined them.

"Did you say something, Margery? Or was it the wind in the chimney."

"I shall . . . marry, that is," said Lady Margery in a firm voice.

"But my dear," wailed Lady Amelia, "just think. All those seasons . . ."

"I only endured all those seasons to please Papa," said Margery in a grim voice. "I shall marry the first man who asks me, provided he is prepared to save my home."

"But how shall you achieve this m-marriage?" stuttered Lady Amelia.

"By military strategy," said Margery with a sudden infectious grin. "I shall amass my feminine weapons and attack."

"But the expense of another season," wailed Lady Amelia. "Where shall we find the money?"

"I shall sell my necklace to the highest bidder," said Margery bitterly.

"And then, dear Amelia, I shall sell myself!"

Chapter Three

When Lady Margery set up her establishment in Berkeley Square, London, she discovered with some relief that her father and his bride were in Paris, where they planned to spend several months.

She had spared herself the expense of hiring new servants by shutting up Chelmswood and bringing the country servants to town. In that mysterious way that servants have of finding out the deepest-laid plans of their employers, everyone from the elderly butler to the knife-boy knew of Lady Margery's scheme for saving her home.

Lady Margery was sitting one morning in the back drawing room, surrounded by bales of cloth and back numbers of *La Belle Assemblée*, since she had plans to make this season's wardrobe herself. The butler, Chuffley, had laid the tea tray on a table in front of the fire, but he still hesitated, standing first on one foot and then on the other.

"You have something to report to me, Chuffley," said Lady Margery, recognizing the familiar symptoms. "One of the servants has been misbehaving?"

Chuffley cleared his throat and looked from the ceiling to the floor. He finally addressed himself to a Chinese pagoda on the wallpaper.

"It's like this, my lady. Me and the others, well, we know why you are in London, my lady . . . to find a husband."

Margery looked amused. "Is that not the ambition of every young lady who embarks upon a season?"

Chuffley looked even more embarrassed. "It's like this, my lady. We all wish you well and . . . well . . . we had the idea that you were planning a sort of campaign. Now, if you were to furnish me with the names of the gentlemen your ladyship was interested in, then me and the other servants could find out interesting things about them which might be useful to my lady."

Margery blushed and accused, "You have been listening at keyholes, Chuffley."

The butler drew himself up. "Chelmswood is an old house and voices carry," he said stiffly. "However, if your ladyship feels I have been impertinent —"

"No, no," said Margery quickly, suddenly touched by this show of loyalty. "We have known each other long enough, Chuffley, not to have any secrets. Servants' gossip about the gentlemen I hope to wring a proposal from would be very useful indeed . . . if you

35

could arrange it in a way that would not put me to the blush."

"Don't be afeared of that, my lady," said Chuffley, his face breaking into a rare smile. "It's our home we'll be saving, same as yours."

Lady Margery crossed to a small escritoire and took out a thick book. "Come here, Chuffley, and I will show you my plan of campaign. Here are three names. First is Viscount Swanley. He is a shy, poetic type of man. Other than that, I don't know much about him. The next is the Honorable Toby Sanderson, a sportsman. I suppose I shall have to learn all about driving a four-in-hand and the art of fisticuffs."

"I shouldn't think so, my lady," said Chuffley. "These sporting gentlemen, for all their tall tales and bluster, are often terrified of the ladies. Mr. Sanderson would perhaps like a lady who was very gentle and feminine and who made him feel very strong and powerful."

"And what about Viscount Swanley?"

Chuffley scratched his powdered head, which, as usual, was itching under its stiff plaster of flour and water. "Poetic gentlemen," he said slowly, "now, they like a sort of managing female. Not bossy, mind, but the type of female who can get a chair in a thunderstorm and make him feel like he's done it himself. Oh . . . and who gives him the impression that all the other ladies are jealous of her for catching him."

"What a font of worldly wisdom you are," laughed Margery. "Now to the third. Mr. Freddie Jamieson, who seems to be a drunk, pure and simple."

"That's difficult, that one," said the butler. "Gentlemen who imbibe too much are always coming across ladies who tell them so and want to reform 'em. I've no advice there, my lady, except to humor him when he's in his cups and speak to him in a soft, gentle voice any time before five o'clock in the evening."

"How ruthless we sound," sighed Margery.

"Not ruthless," said Chuffley. "Practical-like. Why, there's great lords marrying cits' daughters to save their homes. These three gentlemen are as rich as Golden Ball, my lady. But there is another one I might mention . . . the Marquess of Edgecombe."

"No!" said Margery sharply, and then in a quieter voice: "No, the marquess is a rake and I have insufficient experience in dealing with that sort of gentleman."

"I've heard stories," said Chuffley slowly, "that the marquess was not always so. It is said he had a liaison with a certain older society lady when he was a very young man. Treated him badly, she did."

"Oh, no!" Lady Margery put her hands up to her hot face. "Then it is true . . . that he was disappointed in love. And I told him so.

37

I was only funning and wondered why he became so furious."

"In that case, my lady," said Chuffley, "it is well that his lordship is not on your list."

"Just as well," said Margery with a faint tinge of regret.

"There is one other thing, my lady," said Chuffley, hovering near the door.

"Yes?"

"Since this campaign of yours is so important to all of us, my lady, I feel it would be as well to hire a lady's maid."

Lady Margery looked at him in surprise. "But I have my Chalmers. I have a lady's maid."

"Well, now, my lady, Chalmers is getting on, and she never was a *real* lady's maid. More like a housekeeper, I've always thought. Why don't you send her back to Chelmswood and put her in charge of seeing that the place is swept and clean for your return. A *real* lady's maid, my lady, can work magic."

"I have known you since I was a baby, Chuffley," said Lady Margery, "and now I feel I do not know you at all."

"Sometimes old heads are better, if you will forgive the familiarity, my lady. A good general needs the best soldiers in his campaign."

"Very well, Chuffley, so be it. Find me a *real* lady's maid and let us see whether this duckling can become a swan."

As Chuffley left, Lady Amelia walked into the room and sank down on a sofa . . . and nearly did a somersault.

"Tcha!" she said impatiently, "I never can get used to these backless monstrosities."

"It is the latest thing, all the crack I assure you," laughed Margery. "You are supposed to imagine that you are Cleopatra reclining on an Egyptian couch."

"Never mind Cleopatra. I have brought the ribbons and trimmings you desired. Are you *sure*, my dear, that you should be making your own gowns? I am sure you are an expert needlewoman, but will they not appear . . . well, provincial?"

"Not a bit of it," smiled Margery. "I have copied the designs in *La Belle Assemblée* down to the last thread."

Lady Amelia looked at her cautiously. Margery seemed to be so happy and assured. At least they did not need to begin their campaign until the opening of the season, which was a full month away. She voiced this comforting thought and found to her horror that Lady Margery meant to begin her siege that very day.

"I am like the Duke of Wellington," laughed Margery. "I do not hesitate to attack no matter how severe the odds. I wish you to accompany me on a little walk."

Lady Amelia eyed her nervously. "And what am I to do on this little walk?"

"Why, nothing," said Lady Margery brightly. "I will do all that is necessary. The weather, I assure you, is perfect for my plan."

Lady Amelia stared out at the lowering sky. "It looks as if it might come on to rain at any minute."

"Exactly," said Lady Margery.

Viscount Swanley darted nimbly down the steps from his lodgings. The sky was very dark indeed and he intended to make a dash for his club before it came on to rain. He had meant to stay comfortably indoors, since he neither wanted to get drenched or have to battle for a chair or a hansom cab, but one of his footmen had just imparted the news that there was a tremendous wager on at White's right at that very minute. His footman had just received this startling piece of intelligence from someone's venerable old butler, and Viscount Swanley was never one to let a good bet go by.

Two things happened as he reached the bottom of the steps. Heavy drops of rain began to fall and he collided with a very smartly dressed young lady who seemed to have grown out of the pavement in front of him.

He swept off his curly-brimmed beaver and stammered his apologies.

Then he noticed there were two ladies, the younger one being escorted by an older, plumper one.

To his amazement, he realized that the young lady had placed a confiding little hand on his arm. Viscount Swanley was small in stature, but the tiny figure looking up at him made him feel like a giant.

"Oh, please, sir," she whispered, "could you procure a hack for me? It is . . . it is starting to rain."

"Delighted," said Viscount Swanley, although his heart sank to the bottom of his glossy Hessians.

He moved slowly to the edge of the pavement and gloomily raised his cane, expecting the cabbies to drive past him as usual as though he were invisible.

Then he blinked in surprise.

Not only one hack but three came to a stop, including several private carriages. Viscount Swanley did not know that the reason for this sudden halt in the traffic was because Lady Margery was pirouetting round and round on the steps behind him and waving her umbrella frantically in the air.

Margery tripped past the amazed viscount and climbed into the first hack, carefully ignoring the outraged stare of the driver. She turned back on the step of the carriage and looked at the viscount from under her lashes. "Can I drop you anywhere, sir? I am most grateful, you see. No gentleman I have known before has had a commanding enough personality to stop *three* hackney

41

carriages in a downpour."

"By Jove, yes!" said Viscount Swanley, much struck. "I am going to St. James's, so if you could drop me at the corner of Piccadilly, that would be splendid. Charming ladies like you should not be seen in St. James's Street."

He climbed into the carriage and seated himself between Lady Amelia and Margery. Lady Amelia was in a silent state of shock.

"Have we met before?" asked the viscount, enjoying the novelty of having to look down at someone he was talking to.

"Allow me to present myself," said Margery in a little voice. "I am Lady Margery Quennell and this is my aunt, Lady Amelia Carroll."

"Servant!" said the viscount.

The little lady beside him fell silent. The viscount was suddenly struck by a splendid thought: By Jove, she was shy! He decided to draw her out. "Shall you be at the opening ball at Almack's?" he asked.

She raised her eyes fleetingly to his face. "Yes, indeed."

"May I have the first dance with you, Lady Margery?" asked Viscount Swanley, feeling like no end of a lady-killer.

"How very kind you are, my lord. I shall be delighted. I believe this is where you wish to be set down."

"Oh, what! Eh! Yes, yes. Of course. Enchanted. Remember, first dance, what!"

Lady Margery nodded and smiled, and Viscount Swanley ran swiftly down St. James's and plunged into the gloom of White's. He had completely forgotten why he had gone there.

The first person he saw was the Marquess of Edgecombe.

"I say, Charles," gasped the viscount, collapsing into a chair opposite. "You'll never guess what happened. I rescued a lady in distress."

Peregrine noticed with satisfaction that he had succeeded in surprising his elegant friend for once.

"Yes, indeed, and it's no use looking down your nose at me like that. It's true!"

"Tell me all about it," said the Marquess of Edgecombe in a soothing voice.

Viscount Swanley needed no second bidding. "It was like this," he said. "I was coming out of my lodgings and I bumped into this young lady and her companion who seemed to have appeared from nowhere. Well, the young lady asked me to get her a hack, and my heart fell, 'cause you *know* I never can.

"So I held up my cane. Just like this, by Jove, and you would think it was Merlin's wand. Not one but *three* hackneys stopped. You could see the young lady was vastly attractive, because all the cabbies stared at her as if they had never seen anything like it before. Anyway, we shared the carriage as far as Piccadilly and . . . oh . . . I don't know what we said except she has promised me the first dance at Almack's."

"Who is this paragon?" asked the marquess lazily.

"Lady Margery Quennell."

"Lady . . . My dear Perry. You are all about in your upper chambers. Lady Margery is a drab little female who has propped up the wall at Almack's for many a season."

"Can't be the same one," said Lord Peregrine promptly. "This lady is a tiny little thing. Very fetching eyes."

"She certainly must have some mysterious presence," said the marquess dryly, "to halt three cabbies in a downpour."

"Oh, *I* did that," said his friend with beautiful simplicity.

The marquess fell silent and studied the fair and foolish face of his friend thoughtfully.

It was all very strange.

The Honorable Toby Sanderson stumbled out from Gentleman Jackson's Boxing Saloon that afternoon. He felt exhausted. He had tried time and time again to pop a flush hit over Mr. Jackson's guard, with a singular lack of success. Only the day before, the Marquess of Edgecombe had beaten him in a

curricle race with insolent ease. He was tired
and hungry and was beginning to think that
he was, after all, not the splendid sportsman
he had fancied himself to be.

As he stood mopping his flushed forehead,
he became aware of a faint cry of distress
and swung round. The small figure of a lady
was collapsed in the arms of her companion.
Her eyes were closed and she looked about
to faint.

"Oooh! My ankle!" cried a faint little
voice.

The Honorable Toby gave a hunted look
around him, hoping to espy some gentleman
who would leap to the rescue. But the street
was deserted, as most of the fashionable
throng were promenading in the park.

He took a deep breath and stepped forward. "May I be of assistance, madame?"

A pair of gray eyes swimming in tears
looked confidingly into his own. "So stupid
of me," murmured Lady Margery. "I have
twisted my ankle, and my poor friend, Lady
Amelia, is not strong enough to support me
to a carriage. Perhaps, sir, since you seem so
powerful and strong, you could . . ."

Toby puffed out his chest. "Certainly,
ma'am. Lean on me. That's the ticket! Why,
you're as light as a feather. Hey! Cabbie!"

Unlike the response to Viscount Swanley,
cabbies halted immediately at the sound of
the Honorable Toby's stentorian tones. He

helped his fair burden into the carriage.

"Thank you, sir," said Lady Margery, her gray eyes still swimming with tears. "It is not often that one finds such a *strong* rescuer exactly when one needs one."

That was enough for Toby. The female sex were apt to shrink from his strong escort, claiming he talked and smelled of the stables. But, now, this pretty wench showed intelligence and appreciation!

"Escort you home," he said climbing into the carriage. "Can't have a little thing like you struggling out of the carriage by yourself at the other end."

Lady Amelia gave the cabbie the address and Toby looked suspiciously around the carriage and began to sniff. "Damme, if I shouldn't have brought round m'curricle," he said. "This demned wagon reeks of onions. I shall have a word with that cabbie fellow soon as we stop, demme if I don't."

"Oh, please," pleaded Lady Margery faintly. "Please do not make a fuss. I have a terror of scenes. Now, it is different for you gentlemen. You look as if you would not be afraid of *anything!*"

"She'll come unstuck," thought Lady Amelia. "She's buttering the bread too thick."

But Toby looked immensely gratified. "I'm not feeling as strong as usual, ma'am. Just had a round with the gloves with Gentleman Jackson."

46

"Oh, dear," said Lady Margery with an artistic shudder. "Pugilism! It is not a subject for a lady, sir."

"No more it is," said Toby in high good humor. "But we knights have to keep fit in order to rescue fair ladies, eh what!"

"Yes, indeed," said Lady Margery in a gentle voice.

Toby could not quite say why he was so attracted to this stranger. She was wearing a very dashing hat of scarlet feathers which hid most of her face so that all he got a glimpse of was a pair of large tear-filled gray eyes. She was very small, no bigger than a child, and so . . . so . . . yielding, that was the word. He felt about ten feet tall.

It seemed like no time at all before the carriage rumbled into Berkeley Square. Toby sprang down first, and assisted Lady Margery into her house as if she were made of glass.

An elderly butler with powdered hair opened the door and bowed low before the Honorable Toby. "Bless you, sir," said Chuffley in quavering accents. "My mistress is indeed lucky to have the help of such a renowned sportsman."

"You know me?" beamed Toby in surprise.

"Who has not heard of the Honorable Toby Sanderson?" said the butler impressively. "Curricle Sanderson, I believe you are called, sir?"

"Quite so, my man," said the much-gratified Toby, who had never heard the term before, and pressed a guinea into this excellent retainer's hand.

Introductions had been made in the carriage, and Toby realized with some dismay that he should have to take his leave of this warm world of praise and approval. All his life he had stumbled and fled from the female presence, but now he wished very much to see more of the intriguing Lady Margery.

"I say," he said, bowing low over Lady Margery's little hand. "Is it possible I might have the honor of the first dance at Almack's opening ball?"

Lady Margery blushed prettily. "I have promised the first dance to Viscount Swanley, but I shall certainly save the next for you."

"Delighted! Gratified!" spluttered Toby, bowing his way out.

Both ladies collapsed in the drawing room and burst into giggles.

"Really, Margery," protested Amelia, "that *poor* man."

"Pooh!" retorted the unrepentant Margery, "I made him feel no end of a splendid sportsman. And look at all the suffering I went through, sniffing a *vinaigrette* full of onion juice. I thought I *would* faint when he started complaining about the smell. And Chuffley was simply marvelous! 'Curricle Sanderson,' indeed! And that splendid quavery voice."

Lady Amelia looked solemn. "My dear Margery," she protested, "have you considered that you do not seem to hold any of these young gentlemen in any kind of high regard, and yet you are proposing to spend the rest of your life with one of them?"

"I will endure anything to save my home," said Margery grimly. "So far, I have had a successful day, but I have not finished. Ring for Chuffley."

Chuffley appeared promptly, looking well pleased with himself.

"Where shall I find Mr. Freddie Jamieson this evening, Chuffley?" demanded his mistress.

Chuffley took out a small slip of paper. "Let me see," he said. "I sent our potboy to engage Mr. Jamieson's potboy in conversation. Mr. Jamieson has been ordered to attend his aunt's *musicale* this evening. His aunt is Mrs. Mary Divine, who is in residence in Grosvenor Square."

"That *is* a setback," said Lady Margery, removing her feather hat and throwing it on the sofa. "I cannot inveigle an invitation at such short notice."

Chuffley proudly produced a gilt-edged card. "I took the liberty, my lady, of calling at your father's residence at Grosvenor Square. It is not generally known that he is in Paris. Among his correspondence I found an invitation from Mrs. Divine. It is, of course, addressed to the earl and countess but, as you know, it is quite in order for his daughter to accept the invitation and go in his stead."

Lady Amelia groaned and Margery clapped her hands. "Tonight we attack the well-lubricated soul of Mr. Freddie Jamieson!"

The Honorable Toby Sanderson was tooling his bright yellow curricle past the Royal Academy when he saw a familiar elegant figure strolling on the pavement.

"Hey, Edgecombe," he called cheerfully. "Can I take you up?"

The marquess leapt up nimbly next to Toby. "You can drop me at Brummell's. I promised to call and I am already late. You are looking in fine fettle. Did you defeat Jackson at last?"

Toby's face darkened momentarily at the thought of his lack of sporting success and then brightened as he recalled the later glories of the afternoon.

"Never mind about Jackson," he said. "Would you say I was a ladies' man, Edgecombe?"

The marquess twisted in the seat of the high-perched curricle and stared at the beefy face of his friend.

"No," he said baldly.

"Thought not," said Toby with a sigh, "but I mean to learn. I tell you, Edgecombe, when the lady's worth it, a chap will go to any lengths."

"Dear me, Toby, I was not aware of the softer side of your nature. Who is this lady?"

"Lady Margery Quennell, and the prettiest little thing you ever saw."

The marquess stared at his friend in amazement. "It cannot be the same Lady Margery. How did you meet?"

Toby proudly told of the sprained ankle and his rescue and how he had been promised a dance at Almack's.

This was too much for the marquess. "Toby, my dear fellow," he remonstrated. "All the world and his wife knows you don't dance!"

"Hired a dancing master," said Toby, turning a darker shade of red.

"Dear me," said the marquess. "Lady Margery has had a busy day. First she collides with Swanley, who immediately falls under her spell, and only a few hours later she is conveniently swooning in your arms."

"Mind your tongue, Edgecombe," said the normally good-natured Toby. "I don't want to call you out, but damme, I shall, if you go around casting asperates."

"Aspersions," corrected the marquess faintly.

They had arrived outside Mr. Brummell's residence at 13 Chapel Street, and a much bemused marquess took his leave of his friend.

He was ushered into the Brussels-carpeted drawing room, where he could chat with the Beau through the open door that led to his dressing room.

The famous Beau Brummell was attired in a muslin dressing gown and seated facing a mahogany-framed cheval glass with two brass arms for candles. He was sitting in a low armchair waiting for his valet, Robinson, to attend to his hair, which was rather light and thin and needed to be waved with the curling tongs.

"Charles!" cried the Beau, seeing the reflection of his friend in the glass. "Just the man I wanted to see. Have you heard what Charles Lamb is saying about Prinny? No. Then listen."

Brummell waved away his valet and began to declaim:

> "By his bulk and by his size,
> By his oily qualities,
> This (or else my eyesight fails)
> This should be the Prince of Wales."

"Poor Prinny," said the marquess indifferently. "Lord Thanet is calling him 'the *Bourgeois Gentilhomme*' after that fat vulgarian in Molière's play. I am sure he does not deserve such general unkindness."

"Perhaps," said Brummell. "You look worried, my friend."

"I am," remarked the marquess. "There is a certain Lady Margery Quennell who is about to turn up for yet another season. A drab girl in her twenties. This year, however, she has managed to enslave two of my friends in this one day, and the most unlikely two at that!" He told Brummell of the infatuation of the Honorable Toby and of Viscount Swanley.

"You amaze me!" said the Beau. "And you obviously think Lady Margery is deliberately trying to enslave your friends."

"Exactly."

The Beau thought for a minute and then said, "Swanley and Sanderson always follow the fashion. The first time I come across Lady Margery Quennell I shall make sure that she becomes downright unfashionable."

"Do that, George," said the marquess, remembering his own conversation with the infuriating Lady Margery. "The little minx needs a set-down."

Unaware of the plot that was being hatched for her downfall, Lady Margery was preparing for Mrs. Divine's *musicale*. The lady's maid, who had been hired that very day by Chuffley, was a grim Yorkshire woman whose name, Battersby, somehow seemed to suit her appearance.

Battersby had first shocked Lady Margery by announcing that my lady's hair must be cropped. She had then added insult to injury by insisting that my lady's sandy eyebrows and eyelashes should be darkened. Tired of arguing, Lady Margery had at last let her have her way, but warned her that if this transformation did not please, then she, Battersby, would be searching for other employment.

The stern warning left the maid unmoved and she immediately got to work. She then dressed her mistress in a rose-colored muslin gown and fastened the long row of tiny buttons at the back. "You may look now, my lady," said Battersby, holding a branch of candles up beside a long pier glass.

The young, slim, dashing stranger stared back at Lady Margery. Her sandy hair had been cropped so that it rioted in feathery curls over her small head. The darkened eyelashes and eyebrows made her eyes seem enormous.

Margery took a deep breath. She knew the hand of a genius when she saw it.

"Battersby," she said, "I thank you from the bottom of my heart for this transformation. It means more to me than you can possibly imagine."

"Just so, my lady," said Battersby impassively. After all, Battersby knew she was the best, but society ladies were inclined to favor those frivolous Frenchwomen, which was disgraceful when you considered the war was just over. Downright unpatriotic, that's what it was.

She draped a fine Norwich shawl over her mistress's shoulders, and Lady Margery went downstairs to join Amelia.

Amelia's delighted cry of "I declare, we shall succeed after all!" was all the reassurance Margery needed.

The little society world, bounded by Grosvenor Square at one end and St. James's on the other, was a blaze of light from flambeaux flaring outside the houses of the rich. Beau Brummell was in town, and where the Beau went, society followed. Although the season had not yet begun, hostesses were already arranging all sorts of parties, hoping to attract the notice of the Beau.

Although the spring night was warm, Mrs. Divine's mansion retained all the chill of a town house suddenly opened up and not given enough time to air. Lady Margery huddled in her little gilt chair, waiting for the music to begin and regretting that she had surrendered her shawl. Her quarry, Mr. Freddie Jamieson, was sitting quite near. He was sucking the gold knob of his cane and gazing vacuously into space.

Lady Margery was beginning to wonder desperately how she could effect an introduction.

The *musicale* began. A heavy-set German

was howling out what had been described as love songs but seemed to Lady Margery's ears to sound like a series of oaths. She shivered in the cold, occasionally leaning forward to see if she could catch Mr. Jamieson's eye. Her best tactic, she decided, was to claim acquaintanceship with him. After all, he did not seem to be the sort of young man to have any sort of a retentive memory.

There was a short interval, in which they were urged to remain seated, as the celebrated singer would soon be finishing his splendid performance to rush off to another engagement.

Lady Margery leaned forward again. Between her and Mr. Jamieson sat two enormous dowagers. They had loud, opinionated voices, and every time Lady Margery leaned forward they would both cease talking and turn and stare at her rudely from the top of her curly head to the bottom of her little kid slippers.

Lady Margery began to develop a positive hatred for them both.

One was now declaiming to another in a loud voice. "I declare, it's George Brummell this and George Brummell that. Why, the man is nothing more than a popinjay."

The nervous strain of the day was beginning to tell on Lady Margery. She had never been introduced to the famous Brummell but had admired him from afar, liking his well-bred manner and mischievous smile and the way he had introduced the virtues of cleanliness and loyalty to one's friends into a society which had been supremely deficient in both. She fixed the nearest dowager with a hard stare. She said: "Mr. Brummell is an asset to society. His manners are unfailingly well-bred and he does not make cruel, ugly, or stupid remarks about people he has never met."

"Well, *really*," said the dowagers.

"Well done, ma'am," said a light, amused voice behind her.

Lady Margery turned round and looked up into the brown eyes of the famous Mr. Brummell.

There was no time to say anything. The singer was coughing and gargling as a sign that the second half of the programme was about to begin. Mr. Jamieson had fallen asleep and had begun to snore, but nobody seemed to mind, since it added a fitting counterpoint to the guttural songs roaring from the rostrum.

British society always applauds rapturously any form of culture they cannot understand and cannot possibly enjoy. Agonizing boredom is a sure sign that one is hearing something "damned deep." This evening was no exception. Margery had been so busy keeping her eye on Mr. Jamieson that she had actually forgotten the presence of the famous Beau, who had stationed himself behind her.

She rose to follow the others to the supper room, planning to fortify herself for the attack on Mr. Jamieson's sensibilities, when her hand was taken in a warm clasp.

"I am Mr. George Brummell," said the Beau. "May I know the name of the lady who has so gallantly defended me?"

"Quennell. Lady Margery."

"Ah, of course," said the Beau, much amused. "I was speaking to one of your admirers today, the Marquess of Edgecombe."

"The marquess is no admirer of mine," said Lady Margery sharply. "I doubt if he has forgiven me for an injudicious impertinent remark I made last season. It is a pity," she added wistfully. "A friendship with the marquess could have brought me into fashion, and I would *so* like to be fashionable just for one season. I have had so many failures, you know."

"But you *are* in fashion," said the Beau, smiling. "I am taking you into supper, am I not? And *that,* dear lady, is enough for anyone."

Lady Margery realized with delight that she was the center of a certain amount of envious attention.

"I must," went on the Beau smoothly, "do my best to help my champion. Dear me. After all, just look at the dragons you slew for me." He raised his quizzing glass and surveyed the outraged dowagers insolently from head to foot.

Lady Margery gave an infectious gurgle of laughter, and the Beau looked down at her tiny figure in surprise. Why! The girl was enchanting. She really must have said something outrageous to Charles, Marquess of Edgecombe, to disturb that aristocratic gentleman's usual languor.

"Since I am engaged to help you socially," remarked Mr. Brummell when an unappetizing cold supper had been demolished, "is there anyone present you would care to meet that you have not met already?"

"Mr. Freddie Jamieson."

The Beau looked in an amazed way to where Freddie was sneering dismally over a glass of negus and obviously praying to Bacchus for something stronger. "Are you by any chance, Lady Margery, making a collection of originals?"

"Yes," said Margery feebly, knowing that if she told the Beau she thought that Mr. Jamieson was a devastatingly handsome man, she would not be believed.

"Very well," said her escort. "But I will leave you after I introduce you. One second of Freddie's wit is enough for me."

It was an inauspicious beginning. Lord Freddie stared at Margery with gloomy disinterest, obviously categorizing her as just one other part of a curst dull evening.

Lady Margery waited until the Beau had

moved out of earshot and then began her plan of attack. "I see," she remarked in a brisker voice than she had used on her other two targets, "that you are obliged to drink negus. I confess I do not like my wine adulterated with hot water!"

A faint look of animation crept into Freddie's fishlike eye. "You're right," he said gloomily. "Dashed poisonous stuff."

"I think I shall serve myself a glass of burgundy," pursued Lady Margery.

Now she had Freddie's full attention. "By George, Lady M . . . M . . ."

"Margery," she prompted gently.

"Lady Margery. Do you mean to say you have found a vein of gold among this dross?"

"Exactly."

Freddie eyed her suspiciously. Was she going to take him straight to the stuff or was she going to start babbling about music?

He underrated his companion. "Follow me," she said in a firm voice, and Freddie followed, his eyes burning with an unaccustomed fire. Any girl who could wring a decent bottle out of his aunt's establishment was not in the common way.

Margery led him to the far corner of the room where there was a little table screened by some tired and dessicated palms. She rapped her fan across the back of her hand three times, her signal to Mrs. Divine's heavily bribed butler to conjure up a bottle

60

of the best. To Freddie, it seemed to appear on the table in front of him, complete with two glasses, as if by magic.

Margery had hoped that her arrangement with the butler would not have been necessary. But after one look at Mr. Jamieson's singularly lackluster stare, she had been glad of her scheme to fall back on.

Freddie demolished two glasses in a twinkling and then looked across at his companion with something approaching benevolence. "I say, Lady Margery, that's a 'ceedingly fine wine. Thought all you gels preferred negus or ratafia."

"I don't normally drink much wine," said Margery with a friendly, open look, "but I do know that a gentleman detests ladies' drinks."

"You're a right one, 'pon rep if you ain't," said Freddie cheerfully, downing another quick glass. "I must say this stuff simply rolls off the palate."

"Whoooshes over it, more like," thought Lady Margery. "He swallows it as quickly as if it were medicine."

Freddie began to relax. He had never felt so warmly towards a girl before. Girls, in his experience, were apt to lead him firmly away from the bottle rather than directly to it. His companion, he noticed, had an engaging conspiratorial grin. With her cropped curly hair, she reminded him vaguely of a chap in his form at Eton. And when a girl reminds a young man vaguely of the chap he knew at school, then it is a sure sign that the shy young Englishman is well on the way to falling in love.

Freddie was nearing the end of the bottle and already looking hopefully round for more, but Margery did not want him to forget one iota of this important meeting.

She moved into the attack. "I have often found, Mr. Jamieson, that gentlemen who appreciate good wine are often good dancers."

"Quite so," said Freddie, who was in fact an excellent dancer. "I don't wish to seem vain, ma'am, but even the Prince Regent himself commented that Freddie Jamieson could shake a nifty leg. His 'zact words, ma'am. Shake a nifty leg."

"Shall you be at the opening ball at Almack's?"

"I wasn't planning to go," said Freddie. "They've got nothing there stronger than orgeat and lemonade."

"It seems a shame that ladies such as myself should be deprived of a good partner," commented Margery, looking directly into Freddie's eyes.

He began to feel slightly hunted. Then he remembered that, were it not for this little girl, he would still be standing over a glass of negus. And Brummell had introduced her, which meant she must be all the crack.

Freddie made a great decision. "Tell you

what, Lady Margery, I'll come to Almack's just for the pleasure of standing up with you. There!"

Lady Margery looked suitably gratified. To Freddie's surprise, she opened her reticule and took out a small piece of paper and a pencil. "Write it down," she said.

Freddie's mouth fell open and his chin rested on the starched folds of his cravat. "Eh?"

For a minute, Lady Margery reminded him less of his old school chum and more of his former schoolmaster.

"Please write it down," pleaded Margery prettily. "Now, I know a gentleman like you, Mr. Jamieson, will have lots and lots of ladies trying to get you to dance with them. I must make sure you remember your promise."

"Oh, since you put it that way," said the much-gratified Freddie, "I will."

He carefully printed a note to the effect that one dance was promised to Lady Margery Quennell and then tucked it in his pocket. "Keep it next to m'heart," he said with great daring.

His companion did not let him down. She blushed rosily and hid her face behind her fan. "Oh, Mr. Jamieson," she sighed.

By now, Freddie had forgotten to look for another bottle of wine. He felt no end of a splendid fellow. He leaned forward to make another dashing and witty remark and then stared in amazement. His companion had gone.

He looked moodily at the empty bottle and then peered into it as if to see if Lady Margery had been some sort of genie. Then he noticed she had left her fan.

The Marquess of Edgecombe was strolling among the tables at Watier's, wondering whether to go home or whether to settle down to a mild rubber of piquet.

He stopped, amazed, at the unusual sight of his friend Mr. Jamieson, who was sitting in an armchair in one of the corners and fanning himself lazily with a little black lace fan with wrought-ivory sticks.

The marquess sank into the armchair opposite. "Joined the Macaronis, Freddie?"

"Eh, what!" said Freddie crossly, annoyed at having his splendid dream disturbed. "Oh, it's you Charles. Macaronis? Fiddlesticks! Do I look like a Macaroni? Do I wear blue-powdered hair? No. Clocks on my stockings? No. Lace handkerchief? No. Perfume? No. Stays —"

The marquess gently interrupted this catalogue with, "Do you carry a fan? Yes."

Freddie blushed. "Oh, damme — er — this. Belongs to a charming little lady," he said dreamily. "Know who she reminds me of? That little chap in our form — Sniffy — you know, chappie with the yaller hair."

"You're in love," teased the marquess, expecting a furious denial.

To his surprise, Freddie gave him a soulful look and said, "Yes. That's it. That's it in a nutshell. Haven't had a drink since that demned *musicale* of Auntie's, and I feel in top form. Must be love."

Freddie joyfully waved the feminine little fan to and fro in the excitement of his discovery. A faint scent of gardenias escaped from it and drifted across the smoke-laden masculine air of Watier's.

The marquess studied his friend with narrowed eyes. "The lady's name, by any chance, would not happen to be Quennell?"

"That's it!" said Freddie, delighted. " 'Course you know all the beauties," he added gloomily.

"And how did she bring about this introduction?" asked the marquess coldly. "Did she sprain her ankle or faint in your arms?"

"Neither," said Freddie, surprised. "Brummell introduced us. The Beau was uncommonly taken with her himself."

The marquess began to feel that there must definitely be a new Lady Margery on the social scene. This enchantress, who had not only bowled over three of his misogynist friends but had captivated the great Brummell himself, could not be the dowdily dressed little girl who had graced the walls of Almack's so many times.

"Remember last season, Freddie? Remember the last ball at Almack's, I asked you for the name of the girl who was sitting out with a plump lady and I subsequently asked her to dance? You told me then that that was Lady Margery Quennell, daughter of the Earl of Chelmswood."

Freddie racked his feeble memory. "Can't be the same girl," he said at last. "I would have noticed."

"Whoever she is," said the marquess smoothly. "Has it ever occurred to you, Freddie, that you are a very wealthy young man and that she may be setting lures out to trap you into marriage?"

Freddie looked at him for a long minute while he digested this piece of information. He began to get angry. "Look here, Edgecombe," snapped Freddie, "just because you fancy yourself as a bit of a ladies' man, there's no reason to sneer at me. I liked the little lady, 'pon my soul I did, and if you cast . . . cast . . ."

"Aspersions."

"Aspersions at her, I'll have to call you out."

And, tucking the fan carefully into his waistcoat, Freddie stalked out, walking between the tables of Watier's without stumbling for the first time in his life.

The marquess sat for a long time lost in thought. He was very fond of his cheerful,

66

innocent friends. They had all been in short coats at Eton together. He did not want to see them duped by an adventuress.

At last he came to a decision. He would find Lady Margery's address and pay a call. The marquess was well aware of his attraction for the opposite sex. If Lady Margery hoped to trick one of his friends into marriage, then she would have the Marquess of Edgecombe to reckon with. He would make her fall in love with himself. And that would teach the designing minx a well-deserved lesson.

Chapter Four

"Must you do that?" said the marquess crossly.

He was sitting patiently in Beau Brummell's drawing room, waiting for the leader of London fashion to finish his toilette. It was not the extensive barbering that so annoyed the marquess but the fact that George Brummell, not content with Robinson's meticulous shaving, was carefully going over his face with a pair of tweezers to make sure that every single hair was gone.

"My face is my fortune," remarked the Beau, unmoved. "Also my mannerisms, my dress, and my ability to stare duchesses out of countenance. You, dear Charles, are not normally a devotee of my levees. I can see from the martial glint in your cold blue eye that you are excessively put out. What is the cause?"

"Lady Margery Quennell. You promised to reduce her to an unfashionable wreck and instead all London is buzzing with the news that the great Brummell took her to supper and seemed to be enchanted with her company."

"I was," said the Beau, tying his cravat in the *tròne d'amour,* a very well starched style, with one single horizontal dent in the middle; color, *yeux de fille en extase.* "She is not an adventuress, Charles, for I know the breed well. She told me she collects originals."

"That's a damned insulting way to refer to my friends."

The Beau cocked a quizzical eyebrow at him. "Take a damper, Charles. It is not like you to take the opinions of any lady so seriously. I shall not cut her, you know. She has great charm."

"Then I shall deal with her myself," said the marquess, striding from the room and leaving his friend to stare after him in amazement.

It was easy for the marquess to find that Lady Margery was resident in Berkeley Square. An aged butler ushered him into the drawing room and departed to inform Lady Margery of his visit.

The marquess looked round the small but tastefully furnished drawing room and wondered why Lady Margery had not taken up residence in her father's great barracks of a place in Grosvenor Square. It would be a more suitable background for her if she meant to cut a dash.

Perhaps Lady Margery did not like the new countess. After some reflection, the marquess decided that no one he knew much liked the new countess, who was often pointed out as an example that an old family line did not necessarily mean good breeding.

He turned, as the door behind him opened, and got to his feet.

His shrewd eyes immediately recognized the old Lady Margery under the chic new Lady Margery's fashionable exterior. He made her a magnificent bow.

It was really quite a transformation, decided the marquess. The new hair style showed the perfect shape of her small head. The simple sprigged-muslin dress had been cleverly designed in the flowing Empire lines, more suited to a tall beauty. It gave Lady Margery all the charm of a pocket Venus. Her face seemed to have come to life, he decided. It positively sparkled with determination. Lady Margery had found some purpose in life and he believed he knew exactly what it was.

For her part, Lady Margery felt her heart begin to hammer. Dressed in a coat of the finest blue superfine and with a pair of buckskins molded to his athletic thighs, the marquess was much more handsome and disturbing than she remembered. The feminine thickness of his eyelashes only served to accentuate the strong masculinity of his face. He exuded a disquieting aura of arrogance and virility.

She pulled herself together. "To what do I

owe the pleasure of your call, my lord?"

"To the beauty of your looks and the exquisite lines of your form," replied the marquess, with a look which hovered on the edge of insolence.

"I did not think you would talk such fustian," said Margery roundly.

"I forgot," replied the marquess, all mock contrition, "you are not practiced in the art of flirtation."

"I am learning quickly," said Margery dryly.

"So I gather," he drawled. "Three of my friends have fallen victim to your charms, and all in one single day. Four. I forgot about Mr. Brummell. You seem to be a very busy young lady. First you bump into Swanley, then you collapse on Toby, and *voila!* by nightfall, Freddie Jamieson is swooning over you and Mr. Brummell says you 'have great charm.' "

"Did he?" said Margery, momentarily diverted. "Mr. Brummell said that? You must excuse my delight. I am not yet in the way of receiving compliments, you see."

"Oh, you are bound to receive lots more if you continue to be so busy about the streets of London."

"My lord!"

The marquess silently cursed. After all, he had not come here with the intention of making her furious.

He took her unwilling hand in his and gazed into her eyes. "You see, I am jealous," he said simply.

Lady Margery tried to withdraw her hand. She had left the door punctiliously open, but the servants seemed to have disappeared and there was no sign of Lady Amelia. The house was very quiet. The French clock on the mantel gave an apologetic sigh and then timidly chimed out the hours, and a dancing couple on its ornate top creakily whirred as they bowed and curtsied and danced, forever treading out the measure of the hours.

"You are funning, sir," said Margery with a breathless laugh and withdrawing her hand with a jerk, only to find it immediately reclaimed. The marquess bent his tawny head and, turning her hand over, placed a light kiss on her wrist.

Margery felt very young and unsophisticated. She should tap him lightly with her fan and laugh; she should turn her head away and blush. Instead, she looked up at him with her lips slightly parted and her eyes wide and questioning.

Slowly he grasped her by her elbows and lifted her up against his chest and bent his head and kissed her. She stayed rigid in his arms until his lips grew harder and warmer and more demanding. She felt a sudden violent fire coursing through her body, and her lips opened under his while the London morning and the faint sounds of a party of strolling entertainers on the street outside whirled and died away, leaving nothing but a world of passion and dark, dark night.

The marquess abruptly put her from him. His breathing was ragged and he felt like a fool. "You are a witch. A damned witch, Lady Margery. But you shall not add my scalp to your belt."

"I am not collecting scalps," shouted Lady Margery, blushing and furious.

"Oh, no? What about Toby and Freddie and Perry?"

"Are you asking me if my intentions are honorable? Well, my lord, for your information, they are. I mean to find a husband."

"There is a name for ladies like you," sneered the marquess. "Do you intend to kiss all your suitors like that?"

"No," replied Margery with sudden and infuriating calm. "I thank you for the experience, my lord. The next time I shall be prepared to cope with unwelcome attentions."

"It is well known that your father's pockets are to let," said the marquess. "Does this explain your sudden passion for matrimony?"

"My lord Marquess," said Margery coldly. "If you are going to sneer at and despise every lady who comes to London for a season with the intention of getting married, then you may as well go out and insult every debutante in town."

"The Honorable Toby Sanderson," came Chuffley's voice from the door.

Toby strode in and then stopped in his tracks at the sight of the marquess. "Stealing a march on us, Edgecombe, eh?" he asked, not very pleasantly.

"I simply came to pay my respects."

"Don't let me keep you," said Toby cheerfully, holding the door open.

The marquess hesitated. For the first time in his well-bred life he was aware of having behaved badly.

It went against the grain, but it had to be done. He turned and swept Lady Margery a low bow. "My deepest apologies, ma'am."

Margery looked into his blue eyes suspiciously, but there was no trace of mockery there. And after all, she had let him kiss her.

"Your apology is accepted, my lord," she said, inclining her head in a chilly nod in answer to his bow.

The marquess took his leave, and Toby Sanderson experienced the exquisite pangs of jealousy for the first time.

"Better be careful of Charles," he warned, with his rather bulbous pale green eyes popping from their sockets. "Got a bit of a reputation with the ladies."

"The Marquess of Edgecombe was all of the most gentlemanly," replied Margery, and then wondered why she had rushed to his defense.

"Heh! Just as well. Call him out, I would, if he were anyone else."

Margery reluctantly remembered her role as the future Mrs. Sanderson. "Oh, fie, for shame, sir," she said. "The poor marquess having to duel with such a formidable opponent!"

"Well, well, well," said Toby. "Enough of this warring talk. I wondered if you would care to take a turn in the park with me, ma'am?"

Margery found to her horror that the last thing she wanted to do was to spend a sunny morning simpering and flirting with this country squire. But Chelmswood must be saved at all costs.

She demurely lowered her eyes. "I would be delighted, sir."

"Mr. Freddie Jamieson," said Chuffley.

"Hallo, Toby," exclaimed Freddie. "What are you doing here? Brought your fan back, Lady Margery. Wondered if you would care to drive with me?"

"She's promised to me," snarled Toby.

Freddie looked mildly amazed at his friend's belligerent tone. "Don't matter, then," he said cheerfully. "I'll take Lady Margery driving another day."

Lady Margery bit her lip. In her plan of campaign she had certainly thought it would be a good idea to play one off against the other. But she had never envisaged them being in her drawing room at the same time. All it needed was . . .

"Viscount Swanley," said Chuffley.

The three friends glared at each other.

Lady Margery retreated to the fireplace and studied her three possible husbands.

Viscount Swanley was undoubtedly the best looking, in his bottle-green coat of Bath superfine and his biscuit-colored pantaloons molded to a shapely pair of legs. He wore his hair in the fashionable Brutus crop. But his face was dreamy and irresolute and he was already looking dismayed at the wrath of his two friends.

Freddie Jamieson was tall and thin, with dark brown hair carefully curled and pomaded. Although he was only in his late twenties, an early life of dissipation had blurred his once handsome features, slackened his mouth, and placed large pouches under his eyes.

Toby Sanderson was broad, squat, and muscular, with an angry red face which belied his normal good humor. He did not aspire to the heights of dandyism, favouring a drab coat and buckskins laced above a pair of Hessians. A Belcher scarf knotted carelessly at his throat took the place of a cravat, and he had innumerable whipcords tucked into his buttonhole.

Lady Margery made up her mind. Let them fight it out among themselves.

"I am going to change into my carriage dress, gentlemen," she said. "You may decide among you who is going to escort me."

An awkward silence fell on the room after she had left. She had looked unhappy and slightly shaken, which had the effect of making her seem rather the drab Lady Margery of before.

Viscount Peregrine Swanley cleared his throat nervously.

"I s-say," he stammered, "I met Edgecombe at the corner of the street. Told him I was going to call on Lady Margery and he started to laugh. I asked him what was so funny and he said he thought the new sport would be more to my way of thinking."

The angry fire slowly died out of his friends' faces. "What new sport?" asked Toby curiously.

"Oh, it's famous," said the viscount. "You have never heard the like. You run along a street and ring all the doorbells."

"What's so sporting about that?"

"You have to move so fast that no one catches you. Edgecombe said that Dan Whittingham did one side of Albemarle Street in five minutes flat. Butlers and porters popping out all over the place, but he was like quicksilver. Not one of 'em saw him!"

Freddie Jamieson took a deep breath. "Wager you I could do it in under five."

"Whittingham's faster than you," said Toby.

"But he ain't got my length of leg," said Freddie proudly.

"In better trim, though," said Toby. "I'll tell you what I'll do — I'll lay you a monkey you can't beat Whittingham's time."

"Done!" said Freddie.

Viscount Swanley had become quite flushed with excitement. This was even more exciting than when they had all bet on the cricket match between the ladies of Surrey and Hampshire.

"And I'll time you, Freddie," he cried, waving a gold repeater in the air.

"Well, what are we waiting for?" cried Toby.

They all bunched together in a concerted rush for the doorway and then stopped before the impassive figure of Chuffley.

"Gentlemen," said the butler. "Lady Margery is still abovestairs. Are you leaving now?"

All three gave him a hunted look. Did not the man know that Venus herself would be incapable of coming between them and a sporting bet?

"Give her ladyship our compliments," said Toby hurriedly. "Pressing appointment, don't you know."

"Pressing appointment. *Very*," chorused the others.

"Do hurry up," urged Freddie, with the

gambling light burning in his eyes. "We'd better go to White's first and enter the bet in the book."

When the street door had crashed behind them, Chuffley stood scratching his head in dismay.

Lady Margery came down the stairs once more in her pretty new image. She was wearing a grey and white gaberdine dress and a fetching little straw hat with a white veil.

"Gone!" she exclaimed, staring at her butler. "*Gone!* Where?"

"The gentlemen remembered a pressing sporting engagement, my lady," said Chuffley. "They . . . er . . . have gone to ring all the doorbells and knock all the knockers in Albemarle Street."

"What on earth for?"

"The idea, I gather, my lady, is to knock or ring at the door and then run away before one is caught."

"But that is a schoolboy prank."

"No doubt, my lady. But you see, the gentlemen will bet on very strange things, such as which of two geese will cross the road first or which of two flies will climb to the top of the windowpane first. There was even a walking-backwards race to Brighton."

Margery sat down suddenly on the stairs. "But I don't understand. One minute they were glaring at each other and each determined to take me for a drive . . ."

Chuffley gave an apologetic cough. "I happened to overhear Lord Peregrine — Viscount Swanley — explain that the Marquess of Edgecombe had mentioned the idea. The marquess met Lord Peregrine when his lordship was on his way here."

"Just mentioned it, did he?" said Margery with a martial glint in her eye. "I shall not give up my campaign because of the Marquess of Edgecombe."

"I believe a great number of the *ton* are to attend Mrs. Herbert-Smythe's breakfast," murmured Chuffley.

"And you think they will be there. I have an invitation. The battle re-commences this afternoon," said Lady Margery, removing her hat.

The marquess sat in his study in Albemarle Street. He heard door knockers banging and bells ringing all along the length of the street outside, and smiled to himself.

Chapter Five

The marquess, strolling in the grounds of Mrs. Herbert-Smythe's mansion in Richmond, was at a loss to understand his three friends.

They had hailed him exuberantly enough, chattering on about their door-knocking triumph, and Freddie was flushed with victory over having cut nineteen seconds off the Whittingham record. But one by one they had fallen silent and moody.

The marquess suddenly saw the voluptuous figure of Lady Camberwell crossing one of the lawns and hastened to her side to indulge in a little mild flirtation. His friends watched him go with envious eyes.

"It's all right for him," said Freddie, breaking the silence. "He's a Nonpareil, drives to an inch, good man in a bout of fisticuffs, but he's at ease with the ladies as well. He smiles at them . . . so . . . and they fall at his feet. It ain't any fun at these *ton* parties if you ain't got a lady to smile at."

The others looked at him in astonishment at his perception. They had been wondering why they usually felt left out and at a loss.

"Well, let's do something about it," said Toby heartily. "There's the Misses Bentley sitting over there by that rose bush. Dashed pretty gels, both of them. Come along, lads!"

The three strolled self-consciously towards the Bentley twins, who were identically fair and identically foolish.

"Servant," said Toby, bowing low, and suddenly conscious of his wilting shirt-points. "Pretty as a picture, heh!"

Both girls unrolled their fans, cast down their eyes, and blushed. Their names were Rose and Beth respectively, but everyone found it hard to tell the difference between them.

"Oh, Mr. Sanderson," giggled Rose, looking up at him.

Much emboldened, Toby and his friends felt that the nonsense of preliminary compliments was well over and plunged into an account of their morning's adventures. The Bentley girls' smiles grew thinner and thinner until the smiles disappeared altogether like letters being dropped in the postal box.

"Should have seen the Worcesters' Sambo's face," roared Freddie, remembering the black servant's bewilderment.

"Egad!" roared Toby, affectionately thumping his friend between the shoulder blades. "And damme, wasn't old Burtwell's butler hopping mad!"

Viscount Swanley let out a high neigh of

laughter as he relived the morning's triumphs as well. "And d'ye remember old Burtwell himself shouting up and down the street, 'Curst sons of whores, wait till I catch ye — I'll cut your guts to ribbons!' "

All three laughed heartily.

"Mama," whispered the Bentley girls in anguish.

A formidable figure in a hideous turban surfaced from a bench on the other side of the rosebush and lumbered to the rescue.

Gathering her chicks under her wing, Mrs. Bentley faced the three sportsmen.

"How dare you," she roared, turning as purple as her velvet turban. "How dare you soil the ears of my sweet innocents with language fit only for the stables." She raked them up and down with a bulging blue glance and then swept her daughters off towards the house.

The three watched them go in moody silence. "See what I mean?" said Freddie.

Lady Margery Quennell had never before been considered witty or fashionable enough to be invited to such a grand breakfast. But that was before Mr. Brummell had smiled on her.

Margery always considered it rather odd to call such an affair, which began at three in the afternoon and lasted till dawn, a "breakfast," unless of course it was because no one in London society got out of bed before one in the afternoon.

She stood at the entrance to the gardens with Lady Amelia at her side and heaved a sigh of pure pleasure.

Mrs. Herbert-Smythe's gardens were almost as famous as her fortune. Smooth green lawns, arbors of roses, reflecting ponds, rustic benches, and all the other flowers of summer were laid out like a picture to illustrate the perfect English garden.

The Thames wound its green-and-gray way along the foot of the lawns where lines of tall yellow flag iris stood sentinel. The air was heavy with all the scents of early summer — freshly mown grass, thyme, mint, roses, honeysuckle, clover, and bryony. Butterflies performed their erratic dance over the summer lawns and through the golden air.

Beyond the trees could be seen glimpses of the Herbert-Smythe mansion, an early Georgian gem of mellow gold brick.

Chuffley followed Margery and Lady Amelia, his arms full of shawls. He had insisted on accompanying them instead of a footman, and Margery had been glad of her old retainer's offer of support.

She knew also that she was looking her best. She was wearing a daffodil-yellow Indian muslin gown with an overdress of heavy, creamy Valenciennes lace. Her wide-brimmed straw hat had a thick yellow silk ribbon round the small crown and falling down her back in two long streamers. Yellow is usually a trying color, but it emphasized the creaminess of Lady Margery's skin and added gold lights to her sandy curls.

She hesitated at the end of a walk. A light breeze moved across the lawns. All London's fashionable set seemed to be present. It was then that she saw three familiar figures standing at the other end of the walk.

"It's all your fault," said Toby to Viscount Swanley. "You and your curst this and curst that. No wonder they ran away."

"You started it," retorted Viscount Swanley, digging the heel of his shoe savagely into the smooth turf.

"I don't know what's come over us all," said Freddie pettishly. "Demme, we've been here half an hour and we ain't even had a drink."

His friends eyed him with a tinge of respect. Trust old Freddie to get to the heart of the matter.

They were just about to make their way towards the marquee which housed the wine and liqueurs when Toby put a restraining hand on Freddie's arm. He pointed down the walk. "I say, ain't that her? Ain't that Lady Margery?"

His companions turned around and looked. The lace of her dress swirling about her trim figure, Lady Margery came slowly towards them. All at once remembered their behavior of the morning and were about to flee. Then they realized that she was smiling, actually smiling.

She came up to them and said those glorious words, "How splendid to see you all again. You must tell me all about your famous bet."

They looked at her warily. "Do you *really* want to know?" asked Freddie in awed tones.

"Yes, *really*. While I have some tea, of course."

How those three delighted sportsmen bustled about! The amazed guests stared as the three well-known misogynists helped Lady Margery to tea, helped her to cakes, opened her parasol for her, brushed away flies, fanned her enthusiastically, found her a little table at a corner of the marquee reserved for such innocuous refreshments, and then sat themselves down and looked at her with the air of three expectant dogs.

"Now you can tell me all about it, " said Margery.

They began very cautiously and then warmed to their story as Margery laughed and clapped her appreciation. How splendid it was, thought each of the three, to have a young lady to pay court to.

The sun began to set behind the trees and they escorted her over to the marquee where supper was being laid out. They talked and talked until the stars came out. They talked and talked and Lady Margery smiled and waved her fan and listened. They heard the sounds of the band tuning up and busily began to sign their names in her dance card. Lady Amelia relaxed and began to enjoy the evening. Lady Margery's intrigues were not so terrible after all.

Chuffley, standing behind his mistress's chair, decided to go and have a bumper of wine to celebrate, the minute the dancing started. It was surely only a question now of which gentleman Lady Margery would choose.

Occasionally Lady Margery would be aware of the cool blue gaze of the marquess resting on her. She hoped he would ask her to dance, she wished the next minute he would go away . . . she didn't know *what* she wanted.

"Lady Margery is making marvelous progress," remarked Mr. George Brummell maliciously. "Don't you think so, Charles?"

The Marquess of Edgecombe raised his quizzing glass and surveyed the picture of Lady Margery surrounded by her court of admirers.

"It does not worry me, dear George. I can put a stop to that any time I wish."

"How?"

"Watch me, dear George. Just watch!"

He ambled leisurely across to where Lady Margery was sitting and bowed over her hand. He then turned and bowed to his friends.

"Lady Margery is unaware of the great compliment you are paying her," he said smoothly.

"Compliment?" asked Toby curiously.

"Yes. Sporting gentlemen like you, forsaking a splendid bet to entertain this very beautiful young lady."

"Bet!" Three pairs of eyes stared at him. Lady Margery was forgotten.

"You know that little bridge that spans the pond over on the west lawn," said the marquess, waving one slender white hand in that direction. "I heard Gully Whyte betting Harry Trent that only Colonel Dan McKinnon could walk across the parapet without falling in the water."

Colonel Dan McKinnon was famous for his feats of agility.

"Pooh!" said Viscount Swanley. "That little bridge! I could do it in a trice!"

"Care to lay a wager?" murmured the marquess.

"An hundred guineas says Swanley can do it," declared Toby, becoming red with excitement. "And what about you, Edgecombe?"

"I shall stay and entertain Lady Margery."

Margery looked up at him, her eyes sparkling with anger. "But I would very much like to see *you* try this feat, my lord."

"Yes. Hang it all," said Freddie, "you told us about it."

"Very well," said the marquess. "Come, gentlemen." And without a backward glance they marched off, leaving Lady Margery alone with Lady Amelia and quite forgetting that the sets were being already made up for the *rosière quadrille*.

"I am going to follow them," said Margery, getting to her feet. "I know the marquess thought up that stupid bet on the spur of the moment. How dare he try to take his friends away from me. How *dare* he!"

Lady Amelia put a restraining hand on her arm. "You must be guided by me, Margery. It is not at all *comme il faut* to literally run after these gentlemen."

"Then I shall walk," said Margery mulishly, and she started off across the lawn followed by Chuffley, who, despite his loyalty to his mistress was looking forward to seeing a bit of sport to relieve the tedium of the day.

Lanterns decorated the rosebushes and hung from the trees. A perfect full moon rode the clear black sky overhead. It was a night made for lovers, reflected Lady Margery, and *not* for idiotic bets.

By the time she had reached the pond, Viscount Swanley had already removed his dancing pumps and was teetering at the beginning of the parapet in his stockinged feet.

89

His friends were cheering him on.

A crowd began to gather behind Lady Margery, attracted by the noise.

Viscount Swanley did splendidly until he reached the middle of the thin arched wooden parapet. He wobbled, he tottered, he threw one anguished look up towards the heavens, and then plunged headlong into the water. The crowd roared in delight.

"Go on, Edgecombe," said Toby sulkily.

"Go on yourself, Sanderson," yelled someone in the crowd. "Bet you that ton of lard you carry around your middle won't let you do it."

That was enough for Toby. He removed his shoes and leaped up on the parapet with a lightness and agility amazing in so heavy a man. But he only managed a few steps before he lost his footing and hit the water with a splendid splash. The marquess removed his shoes. But Freddie, who had managed to consume several glasses of burgundy during supper, felt game for anything. Exhilarated by the roars of the crowd, and suddenly aware that Margery was watching them, he volunteered to go next.

With the cautious step of the half-inebriated, he reached the top of the parapet, just where it curved, without mishap. After all, he often had to negotiate the pavements of London in the early hours of the morning as if they were a series of tightropes.

Perhaps he would have made it if some wag had not roared out, "Look at the water, Jamieson. Not often you look at water, eh!"

Freddie looked down. The black water shimmered and sparkled with the reflections of hundreds of lanterns and myriads of stars. He began to shake and tremble, he swayed wildly backwards and forwards in an effort to keep his footing. But the damage had been done. He plunged in, and swam to the bank to join his two shivering friends.

The marquess removed his jacket and leapt up onto the parapet. Margery was pushed close to him by the press of the crowd. "I hope you fall," she said in a low voice.

The blue eyes glinted down at her in the moonlight. "But I shall not, my dear lady," he answered, and added in a murmur, "and the object has been achieved after all. My three friends will be obliged to leave the party."

Somewhere deep in her heart, Margery had hoped that he had not planned this mischief. Now she looked up at him with her eyes blazing with anger. He gave her a mocking wave of his hand and set off along the parapet, negotiating it with insolent ease. To a roar from the crowd, he nimbly turned about at the end and strolled back. Then he came to a stop, standing over Margery and looking down at her with a smile of triumph curving his lips.

He made a low bow and his whisper

91

reached only Margery's ears. "After all, my lady, all is fair in love and war."

"Exactly," said Lady Margery grimly. Before he knew what she was about, she had put the pointed end of her parasol under one of his stockinged feet — and heaved. He hit the water with less grace than his friends. He had been near the edge, so he landed in only a foot of water and slimy mud.

Lady Margery turned and pushed her way through the amused and curious crowd. Lady Amelia fussed after her, pointing out that they might as well go home. After all, the gentlemen would hardly be returning all the way to Richmond after they had changed into dry clothes.

But Lady Margery elected to stay. She found to her surprise that Mr. Brummell's approval was all-powerful. She did not lack partners and danced resolutely on the uneven floor until the sun came up. She had believed that the marquess might return. He did not.

She felt immeasurably tired.

During the days before the opening ball at Almack's, Lady Margery had the pleasure of being escorted on various occasions by Toby Sanderson, Freddie Jamieson, and Viscount Swanley.

Sometimes the infuriating marquess would pop up when she was out for a drive with Toby or appear suddenly behind her shoulder when she was walking with one of the other two gentlemen. His presence always meant the end — for the time being anyway — of the gentleman's courtship, whichever one it happened to be. The marquess always had distracting plans for races, bets, cockfights, or mills.

At the end of her tether, Lady Margery called a council of war. It was the afternoon before the opening ball at Almack's and she could see another ruin of a season stretching before her.

She explained the predicament of the marquess to Lady Amelia and Chuffley.

Lady Amelia's plump, motherly face was creased with worry. "I don't know that we can do anything about him, my dear," she said after much thought. "He is exceedingly wealthy. It is a pity he is not enamored of you."

"I would not marry him an' he were," snapped Margery.

The old butler gave her a thoughtful look. The marquess's reputation as a lady-killer was well known, and he feared that for all her protests his young mistress was not immune to the lord's attractions.

"If I may make a suggestion, my lady," he said apologetically. "Perhaps if my lady presented a bolder front."

"Do you mean compromise one of them?" said Margery with horror.

"No, my lady," replied Chuffley. "I mean if my lady were perhaps to be open and honest with these gentlemen and explain the nature of her financial problems and were to say — lightly, mind — that she will be obliged to marry the first who proposes. And then — just a suggestion, of course — if my lady were to hint that one of the other three had *already* proposed and that she felt herself obliged to accept but she would in fact prefer the gentleman she was talking to . . ."

His voice trailed off and the two women looked at him in surprise.

"Play one off against the other," mused Margery. "It might just work."

Lady Amelia let out a squeak of alarm and clutched wildly at her cap. "You cannot do such a thing, Margery. Only think if anyone should hear of it or if the gentlemen confide in each other."

"I don't think that they will," said Margery slowly. "Good man, Chuffley. I shall try this very evening. The Marquess of Edgecombe can hardly start dragging his friends off to cockfights in the middle of Almack's."

Lady Margery could not restrain a trembling feeling of nervousness as she entered Almack's ballroom on the plump arm of Lady Amelia. She wished she had not worn *quite* so daring a dress. It was of scarlet satin with matching velvet insets but cut dangerously low on the bosom.

They had arrived fashionably late and already the heat from the hundreds of candles was suffocating. All the familiar smells of hot wax, sweat, and a hundred assorted perfumes assailed her nostrils. Then the scent of a particularly ripe cesspool floated past her. She gasped and held her handkerchief to her nose. "What on earth is causing that dreadful smell?" she whispered to Lady Amelia.

Lady Amelia looked round and then gave her young companion's arm a comforting squeeze. "Move quickly to windward, my dear," she whispered. " 'Tis only Lord Ellington. Do you know that he asked Forbes-Bennington for a cure for rheumatism t'other day and Forbes-Bennington said, 'My dear chap, you might try changing your shirt.' I declare, Ellington gets riper every season."

Margery found her hand immediately claimed for a country dance by Toby. She plunged nimbly into the dance, seeking an opening for conversation, but it was not until they were prancing gaily round in the *ronde* that she had an opportunity to whisper, "Oh, Mr. Sanderson. A word in private with you, sir, if you please. I am in such distress."

" 'Course," whispered Toby, his bulging green eyes riveted to her delightful expanse of white bosom. How it had stayed covered during all the hopping and bouncing of the dance seemed like a miracle to him.

After the final chord, he bowed and led her over to a small sofa in the corner. "Now," said Toby jovially, sitting down very close to her. "How can I be of assistance, my lady?"

Out of the corner of her eye, Margery saw the Marquess of Edgecombe entering the room and looking in her direction. She would have to be quick.

"Oh, Mr. Sanderson," she breathed. "I am in sore distress. To put it bluntly, I must marry well. My family home, Chelmswood, is about to go under the hammer." She held a wisp of handkerchief to the corner of one dry eye. "A . . . a . . . certain friend of yours has already proposed and I feel obliged to accept him . . . but . . . but I fear he is weak. I need the advice of a *strong* man."

Toby ground his teeth. So either Perry or Freddie had stolen a march on him, eh? Well, he still had a chance. Before he knew quite what he was about, he had proposed marriage himself. She should travel with him tomorrow to meet his mama. He would arrange a small party in her honor. Local gentry, of course. Let her get a feel of her new home. Damme, if he wasn't the luckiest man in the world. For Margery was smiling mistily up at him and breathing a tremulous "Oh, *thank* you!"

Their conversation was interrupted by the arrival of Freddie, who reminded Lady

Margery that she had promised him the Scottish reel.

Toby watched her flitting off on Freddie's arm like . . . "liked a demned fairy," he thought with a sudden rush of proprietary pride. Lady Margery had whispered just before she left that they must keep their engagement a secret for the moment. Feminine nonsense! He wouldn't announce it tonight, of course. But he would send a notice to the *Gazette* first thing in the morning.

A Scottish reel is even less conducive to intimate conversation than a country dance, but when everyone else was getting helplessly tangled up in the figure-eight and Freddie and Margery were laughing and waiting for them to rearrange themselves, she managed to explain her predicament. Freddie's chest swelled. "Marry you meself." She blushed and thanked him and begged him to keep it a secret for the moment. "Of course," answered Freddie, pressing her hand warmly and privately planning to put an end to the nonsense by sending a notice to the *Gazette* in the morning.

It was not often he was able to triumph over his two friends. And Lady Margery would see that an open and aboveboard policy was best. This fellow who had been pestering her with his unwanted attentions — bound to be Perry or Toby — should be put in his place.

Viscount Swanley had the honor of the waltz, and so it was much easier for Margery to converse, although all the time she was aware of the cynical blue eye of the Marquess of Edgecombe. Perry rose to the bait exactly like the others. Like his friends, he had enjoyed the novelty of being able to squire a young lady. Now he would be able to join those mysterious ranks of married men. He was vaguely puzzled as to why he had proposed so promptly. After all, he was a rich young man and various matchmaking mamas had tried every stratagem in the book. He decided that it was simply because Margery was the first female who didn't scare him to flinders. The more he thought about what a good chap she was, the more determined he became to secure the prize. That other fellow who had proposed must be either Toby or Freddie. It would do no harm to post the engagement in the *Gazette* to-morrow. No harm at all.

The Marquess of Edgecombe watched his three friends and decided that love must be a contagious disease. First there was the stocky figure of Toby Sanderson drifting about the room smelling of April and May. Then there was Freddie, who had propped himself against a pillar after his dance with Margery and was watching her with adoring eyes. And now there was Swanley, of all people, twirling around in the waltz and holding that infuriating minx slightly closer than the proprieties allowed.

Lady Margery only stayed for several more dances. It had been a successful and triumphant night. By the force of a formerly hidden very strong personality and a piece of Machiavellian manipulation, she, Lady Margery Quennell, the former drab, had brought three of the season's richest marriage prizes to their knees. She mentally resolved to raise her lady's maid's wages as soon as she was married. But whom should she marry?

She would get to know each of them better against the background of their homes and then decide which would be the least tedious.

She fervently hoped that they would all honor her plea for secrecy. But of course they would. They were gentlemen, after all!

After Lady Margery had left the ball, the three friends found that the dance had become uncommon flat. They elected to stroll to Brooks's for a four a.m. supper of boiled mackerel and then make their respective ways home.

They made a silent breakfast party, each one radiating a strong atmosphere of "if only you *knew.*"

Conversation flagged and they decided to end their night. They lingered outside a cobbler's stall on the corner of Jermyn Street and gave him a polite "Good night." "Good *morning,* gentlemen," said the cobbler, taking down his shutters and wondering what it must be like to be able to stay up till all hours and then sleep until the muffin man's bell in the afternoon.

Toby walked off on his own, his mind busy with plans for the impromptu house party. He espied the tall figure of the Marquess of Edgecombe walking some distance in front of him and hurried to catch up. After all, Edgecombe was patently uninterested in the bewitching Lady Margery.

"I say, Edgecombe," hailed Toby. "Wish me happy!"

"Won a wager?" asked the marquess lazily.

"Won a bride. Lady Margery."

The marquess stood very still. So she had succeeded after all.

"Fact is," went on Toby, "I'm taking her down to meet mother and I'm having a few of the neighbors along for a dinner party. Very sudden, I know, but some feller's been pestering the life out of Margery and I want to get the knot tied as soon as possible. But the locals ain't very tonnish. Care to come, Charles? Add a bit of tone to the party."

"Delighted," said the marquess smoothly.

"Good of you," said Toby simply. "You're a real friend, Charles. I know these country romps don't appeal to you as a rule."

"Anything to help a friend," said the marquess. "I shall arrive around teatime tomorrow."

Toby clapped him affectionately on the back and strode off whistling "Brighton Beach," serenading the morning as merrily as the early birds.

The marquess walked slowly homewards, trying to analyze the conflicting emotions in his brain. He was furious with Lady Margery, but he could not help admiring her for having pulled it off. Her schoolboyish chummy manner had certainly melted Toby Sanderson, who had long claimed that he wasn't in the petticoat line.

Then he wondered if Toby had kissed her. This thought annoyed him so much that he ceased to be analytical and decided to accept Toby's invitation and see if he could not upset her marriage plans in some way or the other.

Chapter Six

The stately home of Lord and Lady Sanderson was within easy reach of London, being situated among pretty acres of woodland in Hertfordshire.

Lady Margery traveled to the Sanderson home, which was called Tuttering, in her own carriage. With her went her two aides, in the form of Lady Amelia and Chuffley. Battersby, the lady's maid, brought up the rear guard with a huge trunk packed with lotions and unguents and various sizes of curling tongs.

"Tuttering is an odd name," said Lady Margery as they turned into the driveway. "It sounds like an exclamation."

"It looks like an oath," said Lady Amelia gloomily as the great early Gothic pile hove into view above the trees. "I declare, it looks like something straight out of Mrs. Radcliffe's novels. Have you read *The Mysteries of Udolpho*?"

"Why, I know it by heart," laughed Margery. "Do you remember the marvelous piece where Dorothée glances within the dusky chamber and utters a sudden shriek and retreats? I trust there will be nothing to afright me like that!"

But when they were ushered into a large gloomy hall, although Margery did not utter a sudden shriek, she let out a little gasp of dismay. It was huge, baronial, and antique.

"Oh, horror!" she whispered to Lady Amelia as the dank chill crept into the marrow of their bones. "They've *washed the walls*. I didn't think anyone did that anymore. They must be terribly old-fashioned."

It had been the eighteenth-century practice to wash the walls before a house party, leaving them dripping wet, but the comfort-loving fashionables of the Regency had put an end to the practice, swearing it caused everything from the ague to consumption.

Toby erupted into the gloom of the hallway. Up till this point, Margery had been wondering how such a member of the *ton* as Toby could possibly fit into this medieval background. But, as he stood there dressed in buckskins and top boots and a drab coat, with something suspiciously approaching a leer on his beefy face, she realized for the first time that he exuded a sort of country-squire brutality quite in keeping with an earlier image of flogging servants and raping the maidens of the surrounding countryside.

"Come and meet mother and father," Toby was saying. "And after you do the pretty, you'll have time to have a rest before dinner."

They followed him silently across the great hall and through a door into a succession of rooms where pretty gilt furniture lay huddled in groups like French aristocrats awaiting the tumbril. The walls behind the whispering tapestries gleamed with iridescent damp, and the trees, pressing against the windows from outside, gave the place the gloomy air of some vast subterranean world.

Like some ghost that had gone deaf with the years and had failed to hear the cock crow, Lady Sanderson sat on a sort of throne on a dais at the very end of a long chain of saloons. She was very hairy. She had gray hair sprouting all over her face, tufts of gray hair peeked out of her ears, and there were even little clumps of hair between her fingers. She was dressed in an old-fashioned *sac* gown which was hitched up to show a bulging pair of ankles tightly laced in a frivolous pair of *glacée* kid boots. The dress was made of some strange type of gray wool, and Margery had a mad idea that she had woven it from her whiskers.

"So you're Toby's gel," was Lady Sanderson's opening speech. "You ain't much to look at. Not like me in my heyday. I was a great beauty. 'Course, I still am," she remarked with innocent pride. "Well, no doubt you'll produce heirs. What d'ye think, Simon?"

There was a long silence.

"Simon," yelled Lady Sanderson, in a voice which could be heard across two spinnies and forty acres.

A panel opened in the wall behind the dais and an older version of Toby's face appeared.

"What, my dear?" asked Lord Sanderson.

"The gel. There! Toby's. What d'ye think?"

"Charming. Quite charming!" remarked the old round beefy face. The panel was slid shut.

"Does that lead to another room?" asked Lady Margery wildly.

"No," replied Toby. "Why?"

"Do you mean," asked Margery faintly, "that Lord Sanderson sits between the walls!"

"Always has," remarked Toby indifferently. " 'Course, he must have come out at some time or else I wouldn't be here, eh, what!"

Both mother and son burst into bellows of laughter at this witticism and Margery and Lady Amelia winced.

"I feel," said Lady Amelia coldly, "that this conversation is not suitable for either the tender ears of my niece or for any saloon."

"Hoity-toity!" said Lady Sanderson, her whiskers bristling with annoyance. "Toby told me you wasn't one of these flibbertigibbets — those die-away simpering debutantes."

Margery opened her mouth to make a cutting rejoinder and then caught Toby's eye. He looked like a guilty schoolboy and threw her a pleading glance. She said instead, "If you will excuse us, Lady Sanderson, we will retire to our rooms. We are fatigued after our journey."

"Take a little stroll in the gardens with me first, eh, Margery?" pleaded Toby. Margery steeled herself. She must be strong. She must tell him that their engagement was at an end. She could not possibly live with such in-laws.

"I shall join you presently," she said to an anxious Lady Amelia, and, laying her hand on Toby's arm, she allowed him to lead her out into the gardens by way of the French windows. They walked sedately along a weedy terrace and then walked down to the thick uncut grass of the lawn.

The sky was heavy and gray and the wind moaned and sighed in the trees. Margery wondered if Lord Sanderson stayed permanently immured between the walls, listening to the sound of the country outside.

Really mad eccentrics were quite common in society. Mad Jack Mytton, the Squire of Halston, had spent half a million pounds in drink over a fifteen-year period, rode a bear around his drawing room, dressed his sixty cats in livery, and shot wildfowl in the depths of winter wearing nothing but his shirt. But, Margery reflected, she had never envisaged becoming part of a family which harbored one of these exotic specimens. Her own father was trial enough, goodness knows!

Toby placed a pudgy hand on hers and squeezed it affectionately. Margery sighed. Now was the time to put a finish to this engagement.

She turned to face him and said gently, "Toby, my dear . . ."

The big beefy face looking down at hers seemed suddenly young and vulnerable, all bluster and swagger gone. The slightly protruding green eyes held a shy, wary look as if he knew what she was about to say.

"Go on, Margery," he said quietly.

Just then Margery noticed a very smart curricle rolling to a stop in front of the house. The Marquess of Edgecombe jumped down and stood with his hands on his hips, looking across at the pair.

"I just wanted to say that I feel very tired and if you don't mind I would like to retire to my rooms," said Margery hurriedly.

A faint shadow of something — relief? — flicked through the green of Toby's eyes and was gone.

"Come and meet my distinguished guest," said Toby heartily. "But then, you know Charles, don't you?"

Margery nodded, faintly aware of the marquess's mocking blue eyes.

"Hey, Charles," said Toby. "Lady Margery is just about to retire. Good idea! Heard the dressing gong just now. But we'll all meet at dinner."

The marquess bowed low over Margery's hand. "My felicitations on your engagement," he murmured. "Toby is indeed a — er — lucky man."

Confused and at a loss for words, she kept her eyes lowered and scurried off into the house.

The great hall yawned on either side of her. She climbed up a hideously carved wooden staircase, which branched off in two directions leading to the first floor. Which way to go?

She then saw the green-and-silver livery of a footman emerging from one of the rooms and, under his direction, she mounted a further flight of stairs and was ushered into a vast bedroom.

When the footman had lit the candles and left, she was at liberty to sort out her confused emotions.

She had thought that life without Chelmswood would be unbearable.

If a rich marriage was the only means of saving her home, then a rich marriage she would have. It had all seemed so simple.

Before the blow had fallen, she had not thought of marriage, simply enduring her seasons until she could get back to the "real" life of Chelmswood. Lady Amelia's placid and uncritical friendship had been all that Margery desired.

Now, what had happened? She was frightened of marriage. If she should marry, then let it be to some congenial companion who would share her interests. Someone like . . . A picture of the marquess flashed before her eyes and she blinked to erase it. The marquess, indeed. The man was nothing more than a mocking *dandy*.

But Margery bitterly realized that there were fates worse than losing Chelmswood or even being a companion to Desdemona. If she suffered Desdemona's patronage, even for a little, then perhaps she might meet some gentleman who would be much more suitable than the amiable but witless three she had just laid siege to. If she could charm them, why not someone else? Someone, perhaps, with little money, but who would not spend his time at cockfights or running amok on mad wagers. Lady Amelia could then return and live with her as before.

Margery tried in vain to imagine a "suitable gentleman," but again the marquess loomed up before her.

What must the marquess think of her anyway — letting him kiss her as if she were the veriest lightskirt? She felt her cheeks grow red with shame and dreaded seeing him at the dinner table.

And how should she tell Toby that she had decided to terminate the engagement? Her head began to ache, but she resolutely rang the bell for Battersby and submitted to her maid's expert ministrations.

Attired in a dark green velvet gown, fashionably low-bosomed and high-waisted and with her hair dressed *à la Sappho,* she timidly descended the stairs and once again walked through the long chain of saloons until she came across the rest of the party.

The party consisted of two of the local county girls who were barely out of the schoolroom — Ann Burleigh and Cornelia Smythe — and three men of Toby's age who obviously shared his sporting habits. They were dressed with obvious discomfort in knee breeches and well-starched cravats and talked in very loud voices about how much they despised the life of London. Lady Amelia was sitting placidly listening to one of them — a Mr. Henderson — rhapsodizing over the joys of otter-hunting. Her motherly face wore its usual look of polite interest, and only Margery knew that she was bored to distraction.

The marquess was undoubtedly the most elegant gentleman there, the magnificence of his bottle-green evening coat and emerald jewelry highlighting the tawdry magnificence of their surroundings. He gave Margery a peculiarly sweet smile, but she resolutely looked away, her heart beating fast.

Ann Burleigh engaged her in conversation. What was London like? She, Ann, would have her season next year. Were the gentlemen very bold? A certain gentleman had helped Ann alight from her carriage only last Sunday, right outside the church, and he had pressed her hand *violently*. Now, didn't Lady Margery think that that was a very *rakish* thing to do?

And Lady Margery wondered what this innocent would think of a passionate kiss from the Marquess of Edgecombe!

At dinner, Margery found to her horror that she was expected to make a speech on her engagement. She blushed and claimed to be over-tired from her journey and earned a contemptuous "Pooh! Fiddlesticks!" from Lady Sanderson. No one asked or seemed to care about Lord Sanderson. It was almost as if he were dead, decided Margery.

There was no respite after dinner. Toby suggested that the gentlemen should join the ladies immediately instead of lingering over their wine.

He would entertain them with a song he had just learned by heart. Margery was pressed into service at the pianoforte while Toby stood beside her, leaning uncomfortably close.

She nearly jumped from her seat as Toby began to roar out his song with all the finesse of an anguished bull:

"I'm come a lusty wooer,
My dildin' my doldin',
I'm come a lusty wooer,
Lilly bright and shinee . . ."

111

The song seemed interminable, and, as is the way at these home *musicales*, the guests merely endured the first stanza before turning round and talking to each other. Margery alone was left to endure the brunt of the dildin-doldins, and Toby breathed passionate brandy fumes over her at the end of each line.

At last it was finally over and the voice had stopped. Margery looked up at Toby in a bewildered way, as if she could not quite believe that her ordeal was over. When she realized that it was indeed finished, she gave Toby a dazzling smile of relief and gratitude, which the closely watching marquess interpreted as love.

"Well, that's that," thought the Marquess of Edgecombe, giving a vicious kick to the logs in the fire. "She does love him after all, therefore I have no reason to stop her from wedding Toby." And then he wondered why that cheering thought should make him feel so savagely gloomy.

Toby was now pressing Margery to entertain the company. She selected a very long composition by Scarlatti and resolutely began to play. If she played, she would not have to talk or think.

A whole hour passed and the guests began to fidget and yawn and only the marquess realized that Margery was playing the same piece of music over and over again.

Lady Sanderson began to grumble behind her whiskers and then suddenly sprang into action. She picked up the nearest cushion and hurled it at her son's head. "A romp! A romp!" screamed the two young girls, leaping joyously from their chairs and beginning to throw cushions at the young men. The young men retaliated with apples and oranges, and Ann and Cornelia threw down their cushions and let fly with candlesticks and *objets d'art.* Margery stopped playing and turned round.

Lady Sanderson was roaring with laughter, her face a weird purple behind its barrier of whiskers. Lady Amelia was hiding behind the curtains. The marquess had retreated to a corner of the room and was watching the scene, his face a mask of boredom.

"Let's smother the ladies," roared Toby, advancing on Lady Margery with a cushion. There were whoops and cries all round. Ann Burleigh had climbed up on a sofa and was displaying an unmaidenly glimpse of leg. Margery took to her heels and fled with Toby yelling, "Yoicks! Yoicks!" and pounding behind her.

She ran swiftly through the seemingly endless saloons. The butler was standing on the front step with the great door of the hall lying open.

Margery fled past the startled butler and out into the grounds. The grass was soaking wet from a heavy fall of dew. Her slippered feet were soaked through in an instant, but, undeterred, she ran and ran, across the great uncut lawns to the safety of the Home Wood, where she collapsed sobbing for breath against a tree.

It was a brightly moonlit night and, peering round the trunk of the tree and through a gap in the wood, she could see the heavy figure of Toby, his great bull-like head twisting this way and that. Then the other guests crowded onto the lawn behind him.

"A hunt for Margery!" Toby was crying. "Bring torches!" The servants came out and handed each guest a flaring torch, and with great whoops and cries they spread out over the grounds.

Margery did not want to be caught. She had always managed to avoid these romps in the past and even left the room when anyone suggested blind man's buff. She was frightened of being found and facing a circle of jeering faces. These romps were usually an excuse for the gentlemen to get their arms around the ladies and could end in accidents.

Margery remembered attending a formal dinner at Woburn the previous year. During dinner, everyone whispered to his next neighbor and Margery had been frightened of the sound of her own voice. After dinner, the guests dispersed throughout the saloons, some to play the harp or take up an attitude on a sofa or play cards or talk of furniture.

The Duchess of Bedford suddenly entered at the head of a troupe of young men and women. They had started throwing cushions. Then everything was thrown. The romp was at last ended by the duchess's daughter, Lady Jane, being nearly blinded by an apple which hit her in the eye, and the poet, Shelley, had been nearly smothered by the female romps getting him to the ground and pommeling him with cushions.

The whoops and halloos of the searchers drew closer, and Margery began to look wildly round. She seemed to be surrounded. There was only one way to go. Up.

Hitching up her skirts, she climbed nimbly up the tree as far as she could go and then settled herself comfortably on the fork of a branch and waited for the search to end.

The night was damp and humid and she began to shiver in her now-bedraggled dress. Suddenly it was quiet. She could no longer see the flare of the smoking torches between the trees. Margery eased her cramped limbs and prepared to descend. Then she froze as she heard the sound of voices directly underneath her. It was Toby and one of his friends, Jeremy Byles. Toby's exasperated voice rose clearly in the still air. He said: "Demme, Jeremy, but this is beyond a joke, upsetting m'household like that. M'mother says there's something strange about her."

"Never thought to see you gettin' leg-shackled," said Jeremy.

"Never thought to see it meself," said Toby sourly. "I wish now . . . Well, never mind."

"Can't expect a man to go through with it if the gel's insane," Jeremy's voice suggested.

"Well, you know how it is," said Toby. "I never know what to say to the ladies — and Margery, well, it's like talking to another chap, you know. Easy going. Never a suggestion of anything wrong with her till now."

"Not as if she's a real dasher, either," said Jeremy.

"She looked different in London," said Toby slowly. "All smiles and sparkle. She looks quiet and worried now and it takes a bit of the shine off."

"It ain't as if you've got to get hitched," persisted Jeremy. "No reason, eh?"

"You mean, have I thrown a leg over her?" said Toby with brutal frankness. "No. Not yet I ain't."

"Tell you what I'll do," said Jeremy. "Anything to help a friend. I'll hint her off, you know. Say you've got the pox."

"I say, steady on," howled Toby, his voice shrill with alarm.

"Oh, well, I could say you were secretly in love with someone else."

Toby suddenly remembered how, a few years ago, he had been charmed by one of the local county girls and had confided as much to Jeremy. And how this Jeremy had gone on and on and *on* pointing out the many disadvantages of marriage. Dammit! He had made the whole idea of getting married seem like a foppish action.

"Don't do anything until I speak to Margery," he said curtly. "No use standing here getting wet feet. She's probably in her rooms."

Margery found she was trembling with rage. How *dare* Jeremy Byles interfere? Then she remembered that she no longer wanted to be affianced to Toby and that the infuriating Jeremy did not know that she had been sitting directly above their heads.

Stiff and cramped in every limb, she climbed down from her hiding place and walked wearily towards the house. All was quiet. The moon silvered the wet grass and sparkled on the dewdrops hanging from the thorns of the tangled rosebushes. Somewhere an owl hooted, opening up vistas of lonely empty countryside.

A shadow detached itself from a pillar of the porticoed entrance.

"The party is over, Lady Margery," said the light, mocking voice of the marquess. "You do not show the courage I expected — to flee before a party of rowdy romps."

"I do not like romps," said Margery stiffly, feeling very young and pompous. " 'Tis an unfashionable trait, I'll allow."

He walked beside her into the hall. The

candles had been snuffed and the great hall was lit by the red glow of a dying fire.

Margery hurried towards the staircase, but the marquess put a restraining hand on her arm.

"Stay for a little," he said in a more gentle voice than she had ever heard him use before. He drew her gently towards the fireplace. Margery sat down on a high-backed settle and looked up at him apprehensively. He sat down opposite her, his face half hidden in the shadows. He threw a log on the glowing embers and the flames leapt up, sending eerie shadows wavering and dancing round the walls.

"I have already apologized to you, Lady Margery," said the marquess in a husky, hesitant voice. "I now feel I owe you another apology. I had damned you as an opportunist and I thought that you had no affection in your heart for any of my friends. But when I saw you look up at Toby this evening, I realized that your emotions were genuine. Also, it must be a bitter blow to be faced with losing one's home."

Margery felt tears start to her eyes at the unexpected sympathy in his voice. She longed to confide in him; to tell him that she didn't care a rush for any of his friends. But how he would despise her!

"Perhaps," said Margery, staring into the flames, "I loved Chelmswood too much. It is only bricks and mortar, after all.

"There seemed to be no discomfort to cope with. I had Amelia's undemanding and uncritical friendship and I lived through the lives of my tenants."

The marquess listened silently, one long hand laid against his thin cheek. He had a feeling that she was talking more to herself than to him.

Margery went on after a short silence. "Yes! That was it! I lived the lives of my tenants. Their marriages were my marriage, their babies my babies, their illnesses my illnesses, but . . . oh . . . all comfortably second-hand . . . like reading a thrilling book. Father was mostly away from home. The only time I ever had to step into the real world was when I had to face another season. I enjoyed looking as unattractive as possible. That way I *knew* nobody would ask me to dance and I could therefore save myself from the pangs of rejection and failure. Each season was like a bad dream, to be endured with patience until I could return to Chelmswood and wrap myself in the minutiae of its domestic affairs and tenants' problems. I wonder now whether it all kept me too young for my years."

"And you so ancient," teased the marquess. "But," he added bracingly, "*this* will soon be your home."

Margery started and looked wildly round as if awakening from a bad dream. "This!"

she said in a horrified voice, which seemed to encompass everything from the neglected park to the damp rooms to the elderly lord immured between the walls.

"Of course," replied the marquess, surprised. "You will naturally live in your husband's home. You did not think you could possibly get married and then simply return to Chelmswood?"

Lady Margery raised her hands to her face. That was, in fact, just what she *had* thought. She began to wonder if there were insanity in the family. But . . . but . . . perhaps one of the other two suitors would not be so bad . . . but . . . but then he would expect her to share his life and . . . and . . . his bed.

The marquess watched the changing emotions flickering across Margery's little face. She looked like an agitated pixie, her tiny figure perched on the huge settle and her slippered feet barely touching the floor.

"You *are* in love with Toby, aren't you?" asked the marquess with sudden curiosity.

Margery's eyes flew to his face and then dropped again in confusion. The marquess once again seemed a hard, cold stranger whose mocking eyes shone queerly in the dancing light of the flames.

"You must excuse me, my lord," she said, getting to her feet. "The hour is late." She dropped him a curtsy and hurried off into the darkness of the staircase before he had realized that she had not answered his question.

The marquess sat for a long time looking into the fire. He felt rather sad and . . . and . . . *desolate* . . . that was the word. It must have been too much burgundy at dinner. How strange the workings of one's liver! How strange that a couple of bottles of Toby's best should make the world seem such an empty, endless desert! He would go to the library, where he had last seen a bottle of Mr. J. Schweppes' soda water, and drink the lot.

Margery awoke to blazing sunshine and a blinding headache. From the clamor of birdsong outside the window, she realized it must be too early for the eleven o'clock breakfast. She would take a walk downstairs and indulge in the unfeminine practise of reading the morning papers.

She passed various servants going about their duties on her way downstairs, but there was no sign of the other members of the household.

She stopped the butler, who was crossing the hall, and asked him if the morning papers had arrived. He inclined his powdered head in assent and said they had been given to Lord Sanderson, who often threw them out into the end saloon after he had finished with them.

Margery wandered through the empty

rooms until she came to the end one. Lady Sanderson's "throne" was empty and an elderly dog — the only occupant of the room — lay snoring and whooping on the sofa as it chased rabbits across the endless fields of sleep.

Lord Sanderson's panel was closed and there was no sign of the newspapers. Margery was just about to leave when the panel in the wall slid open and Lord Sanderson's head popped out with the effect of a jack-in-the-box. He was wearing a nut-brown wig, which was slightly askew. Margery reflected how odd it was that white wigs or gray wigs, however badly made, gave their wearer a certain dignity, but brown wigs always bestowed a certain air of madness, even on such a personage as the Prince Regent, who had recently been seen wearing one. Then she noticed that, wig apart, his lordship was certainly behaving in a very strange manner. One chubby finger was laid alongside his bulbous nose and he was unmistakably leering.

"Come into my study," invited Lord Sanderson, ogling her horribly.

Margery wondered for one wild minute whether she was meant to climb through the small opening, which at the moment was filled by Lord Sanderson's great red face.

"How do I get there? Your study, I mean," she faltered.

There was a whirring of some antique clockwork mechanism and a section of the paneling opened to reveal a small entrance.

Feeling somehow that she would do better to turn and run, Margery nonetheless edged through and found herself in a small cubicle, almost pressed up against Lord Sanderson. To her relief, the mechanism whirred again and another small door opened in the wall opposite. Lord Sanderson led the way into a surprisingly cozy study. The curtains were tightly drawn, but a cheerful fire blazed on the hearth and two large rose-shaded oil lamps cast a comfortable glow.

He was not so eccentric after all! Admittedly the cubicle between the walls showed more signs of occupation than the study, which must have been the reason Toby had led her to believe his father spent his whole life walled up.

Her apprehensions gone and now feeling amused and slightly indulgent, Margery smiled at his lordship and said, "What was it you wished to discuss with me?"

"You're a one, ain't you?" said his lordship, with the same horrible leer as before. "Hot as mustard, you are. Ain't no doubt about that!"

Lady Margery drew herself up to her diminutive height. "You are abusing your position as a host, my lord. Pray conduct yourself in a more seemly manner."

"Ho! Miss High and Mighty." The leer was wiped from Lord Sanderson's face, to be replaced by the malicious look of a spoiled brat. "There ain't any *lady* of my acquaintance who gets herself engaged to three gentlemen on the same day!" Lord Sanderson brandished the newspapers in front of Margery's bewildered face. Impatient with her seeming stupidity, he thrust the *Gazette* in front of her eyes. There, staring up at her, the black print seeming to leap out of the page, were three engagement notices. For all the world to see, Lady Margery Quennell was engaged to Toby Sanderson, Freddie Jamieson, and Viscount Swanley.

"I didn't mean . . . I d-don't know what c-can have h-happened," stuttered Margery, backing away.

"That's what all the lightskirts say," said Lord Sanderson. "I know the world. I stay shut up here so's to keep away from *her* and her fat feet and hairy face. But certain times I go down to the village to get a bit of young flesh. I'm still the lord 'bout these parts, heh! Respect the ladies, but the trollops? Let 'em scream and yell. There's worse in life than to be mounted by me, heh!"

He was advancing on her. His wig had slipped completely to one side in his excitement and his shaven head gleamed in the rose light.

Margery looked wildly round for a means

of escape. Lord Sanderson's pudgy hands were stretching to the fastenings of her dress. She turned and banged furiously on the wall. Miraculously both doors slid open and Margery catapulted through, but not before she had left a sizable piece of her muslin dress in Lord Sanderson's beefy hands.

Once again she was fleeing through the chain of saloons, but this time she was screaming for help at the top of her voice as Lord Sanderson lumbered after her.

Suddenly everyone appeared at once. She collided with the fat bulk of Lady Sanderson and sat down with a thump on the floor. The startled faces of Toby, the marquess, and Lady Sanderson gazed down at her.

Lady Sanderson was the first to recover her wits. She glared from the white face of Margery to the beefy hand of her husband, which was still clutching a piece of muslin.

"Strumpet!" she yelled at Margery.

"Hold on!" The cold voice of the Marquess of Edgecombe cut off whatever further Lady Sanderson was going to say. "I think Lord Sanderson owes us all an explanation."

"That's a fine one," said Lord Sanderson. "I'm in my own manor and on my own land and a lightskirt is a lightskirt."

"If I didn't think you were quite mad," said the marquess, "I would call you out, despite your age."

"I'll show you what kind of woman she is,"

spluttered his lordship. "Come along!" They trailed after him to his study, Margery holding the rags of her dress round her.

In silence, Lord Sanderson handed them the *Gazette*. In silence three pairs of eyes looked at it and then turned and stared at Margery.

The marquess was the first to speak. "This *must* be a practical joke," he said with a reassuring smile.

Distraught with shame and worry, Margery blurted out, "But I *told* them *not* to announce the engagement. I didn't mean . . . I didn't know . . . I hadn't made up my mind which of them I would marry."

The look of distaste and contempt on the marquess's face made Margery recoil as if he had struck her.

Toby Sanderson had forgotten all about ending his engagement. His friends had stolen a march on him — had made a fool of him. He felt as if he had caught them cheating at cards.

He made Margery a clumsy bow. "Your honor shall be avenged, my lady," he said and strode from the room.

"Don't be a fool, Toby," yelled the marquess. "It was all her fault!"

Their voices died away to a murmur. Lord and Lady Sanderson stared at their young guest with baleful eyes.

Lady Margery became aware that Lady

Amelia was standing at the entrance to the room. Amelia walked forward and put a comforting arm round Margery's shoulders.

"Come, dear," she said. "We shall pack and leave immediately."

"She ain't leaving nohow until we get an apology," snapped Lady Sanderson.

Margery had never known Amelia to be anything other than a motherly, tranquil person. Now a new Amelia emerged. With gray eyes as hard as frost, she stared down at the ruin of Margery's dress and then at Lord Sanderson until he dropped his eyes.

"You deserve to be horsewhipped or put on show at Bartholomew Fair with the other freaks," she said in a voice that dripped acid. "You will inform the servants that we are leaving, and if you so much as interrupt my progress, I shall not be responsible for my actions."

She drew the trembling girl from the room and left my lord and my lady staring after her in surprise. They felt as if some pet hound had suddenly bitten them in the ankle.

Chapter Seven

The white-hot heat of rage that had carried Toby posthaste to London had also carried him straight to Watier's, where he found Freddie playing hazard. His hand seeming to move of its own volition, Toby struck his friend across the face and demanded satisfaction. He would kill Freddie first and deal with Perry afterwards.

His rage had carried him through a restless night and through the dark ride to Chalk Farm in the early hours of the morning, where he was to meet Freddie.

Now he would have given anything for one particle of that splendid rage to sustain him.

It was as beautiful a morning as a man could wish to see. Golden sunlight sparkled on the dew-laden grass and burned in diamonds on the spiders' webs. Daisies starred the grass, opening their petals to the warmth of the sun. Quite near him, blissfully unaware of the violent world of men, a robin fought gallantly with a large worm. A hawthorn tree stood in the center of the field, a bridal miracle of white blossom. To Chaucer it was a sight that "fills full the wanton eye with

May's delight" but to Toby Sanderson it seemed like a white ghost come to mock the folly of one hotheaded London guck.

Toby wished Freddie would hurry up before the tide of memories threatened to engulf him. What sport and larks he and Freddie had kicked up together. Now, in a few minutes, they would be facing each other in all the glory of the summer's morning, each attempting to put a ball through the heart of the other. Insanity!

Well, at least he, Toby, was a poor shot. Nonetheless, he would delope. Freddie should have the honor of killing his man.

Toby heard the clatter of horses' hooves. His seconds had arrived. Then all too soon came the carriage with the surgeon, then Freddie himself, followed by Viscount Swanley and the Marquess of Edgecombe.

Both men measured their distance. The handkerchief fluttered to the ground. Both men deliberately raised their weapons to fire into the air. But Toby, who could not have hit a barn door were he pointing his weapon straight at it, by trying desperately to miss his friend by miles succeeded in hitting his target for the first time in his life.

Freddie stood swaying on his feet, his mouth hanging foolishly open in surprise, before he fell headlong on the grass, the blood from his wound gushing over the grass and staining the daisies crimson.

Toby fell to his knees. Great racking sobs tore themselves from his chest and shattered the summer silence like obscenities. Then he was dimly aware of the marquess shaking his shoulder and saying, "It's all right, d'ye hear? *It's all right.* I think Freddie has a flesh wound and that it looks worse than it is. The surgeon's binding him up, and it won't do him any good to hear you going on as if you're at a funeral."

Toby dried his eyes on his sleeve and let the marquess help him to his feet.

"We must make sure that this duel is not made public," said the marquess sternly. "Do you hear me, Toby?"

Toby drew a shaky breath. "You mean because we must protect Lady Margery's reputation?"

"Lady Margery's reputation be damned," said the marquess wrathfully. "I mean yours and Freddie's. I would not have it known that you fought over such a . . . a *scheming drab.*"

Three weeks had passed since the unfortunate duel, and Lady Margery felt as if she were convalescing after a great illness. Guarded by the ever-vigilant Lady Amelia, she had seen no one although many had called.

A notice had been placed in the *Gazette* explaining that the three engagements had been a mistake, London found other things to gossip over, the duel was kept secret even from George Brummell, and Lady Margery Quennell remained fashionable.

With the resilience and optimism of youth, she began to recover quickly and to hope that her father had forgotten about selling Chelmswood. Mr. Jessieman had sent word to say that he had had no further instructions regarding the estate.

Amelia began to agree with her young friend that perhaps they had driven themselves into a pother over nothing and that it could be as well to retire to Chelmswood and conserve the rest of their money instead of frittering it away on a frantic hunt for a husband for Margery.

Amelia announced her intention of setting out for Chelmswood to see that all was in preparation for Margery's return. Margery should follow in a few days' time at her leisure. Lady Amelia did not feel it necessary to caution her young friend to keep to the town house. Margery still seemed to be disinterested in going back into society.

Lady Amelia had no sooner departed than Margery began to miss her constant presence and reassuring friendship. She felt on edge and restless. The sun blazed down day after day. The faint sound of music from balls and parties at the neighboring mansions filtered through the open windows on the evening breeze. The Marquess of Edgecombe must still be there somewhere in that fashionable world. Would he still look at her with scorn, or would he talk to her in that gentle voice he had used when they had been sitting before the fire that night, after the romp?

A gold-embossed invitation to a supper at Carlton House propped against the drawing-room mirror caught Margery's eye. She had accepted it but now did not feel she had the courage to go, without the comforting chaperonage of Lady Amelia, and she had done nothing about finding another suitable lady to escort her.

On the day of the supper at Carlton House, Margery had just finished supervising her packing when Chuffley announced a caller. Mrs. Mary Worthey sailed into the room before his announcement had died away.

Mrs. Worthey was a wealthy widow who had busied herself during the early part of the season by buying her way into the best households. By great contrivance, she had secured an invitation to Carlton House. She did not wish to go with her usual unfashionable companions and, having heard that Lady Margery was all the crack, had decided to call to see if she could ingratiate herself into the good graces of this latest social star.

She was a tall, thin, angular woman, much rouged and powdered. Her dress was daringly damped, after the latest fashion, to reveal the scrawny charms of her middle-aged body. Youthful ringlets of an improbable shade of gold peeped out from underneath a frivolous bonnet in a screaming shade of pink. Her parasol had a handle as long as a Macaroni's walking cane, and her gown, which was cut daringly short, showed bony ankles lashed into Roman sandals.

What was the purpose of this visit? Why, she had heard that *dear* Lady Amelia was out of town and wasn't Edgecombe just saying to her the other day that poor Lady Margery would be in need of a chaperone an' she wished to attend Carlton House?

Now, Mrs. Worthey had picked the marquess's name out of the hat of her imagination at random. She could just as well have mentioned Sally Jersey or Brummell or Lord Alvanley or, for that matter, the Prince Regent himself.

Had she mentioned any other name, Margery would have perhaps seen the woman for what she was — vulgar, lying, and pushing.

But the marquess's name suddenly endowed Mrs. Worthey with a glamor she did not deserve. On her entrance, Margery had been shocked at the vulgarity of Mrs. Worthey's dress. Now she assumed that she, Margery, was out of touch with the very latest mode.

Yes, Lady Margery would be delighted to accept Mrs. Worthey's escort. *Too* kind. Mrs. Worthey was an old campaigner. Having secured Margery's promise, she hurriedly took her leave. She had too often made the mistake before of outstaying her welcome when her victim, no longer bedazzled by the stream of familiar and famous names, suddenly saw beyond them to the character of the woman herself.

So it was with some misgiving that Lady Margery took a cool, appraising look at her new friend as they set out for Carlton House that evening. Mrs. Worthey had so much white paint on her face and black paint round her eyes that she looked like a mummer. Jewels of every description were scattered about her person. She reeked of a mixture of old sweat, old perfume and new perfume, and burning hair where her maid had been overzealous in heating the curling tongs.

After one fastidious shudder, Margery retreated into the comfort of her thoughts. The marquess had mentioned her name. How odd that someone so fastidious should consult Mrs. Worthey. She looked like a Covent Garden abbess!

But he *had* thought of her. And Margery could not quite understand why a ray of sunshine seemed to have penetrated the gloom of her life.

But as she turned a deaf ear to Mrs. Worthey's prattling, Margery suddenly realized that she was more than likely to have to confront her three former fiancés, and only the hope that she would be seated away from them kept her from turning back.

Margery was wearing the regulation court dress of black muslin over an underslip of rose sarcenet. Mrs. Worthey was similarly attired, except that she had achieved the almost impossible effect of making the formal court dress look positively indecent.

There were about two thousand guests milling around the rich splendor of Carlton House. The main supper table filled the two-hundred-foot length of the Gothic conservatory.

To Margery's relief, Mrs. Worthey was ushered to a place at a table in the garden reserved for the less-distinguished guests. She herself was placed quite near the important center of the table, with an elderly peer who seemed half asleep on one side of her and Tom Moore, pet poet of the Whig aristocracy, on her other. There was no need to search for a conversational opening. Mr. Moore burst into a rapt monologue wherein he gasped and exclaimed over "the gorgeous scenery, the assemblage of beauty, splendor, and profuse and magnificent . . ." Lady Margery began to relax and to enjoy being back in society.

In front of the regent's seat was a large circular basin that fed a stream which flowed through banks of flowers down to the end of the table, and Margery noticed with delight that live gold and silver fish were swimming up and down in this artificial river. The prince was wearing the uniform of a field marshal — which he was entitled to do since he had just appointed himself one — and the seams of his gorgeous uniform were heavily embroidered.

There were hot soups and roasts, cold food, peaches, grapes, pineapples, and other out-of-season fruits piled up in great mounds. And, apart from the bewildering variety of wines, there was iced champagne for everybody. All the tureens, dishes, and plates were of silver.

Margery had heard some muted grumbles over the horrendous expense all this magnificence must be costing the country. Shelley had estimated the cost at 150,000 pounds, but others pointed out that the figure was surely exaggerated, and after all, the poet might be suffering from pique since he had not been invited.

Tom Moore ceased his eulogy and applied himself with equal energy to his food. Then a familiar drawling voice seemed to cut through the babble and Margery felt her heart leap into her throat.

"I am amazed," said the familiar voice of

the Marquess of Edgecombe, coming from somewhere down the table near the royal presence, "that this social gathering is graced by the dubious honor of the presence of Lady Margery Quennell."

There was a shocked silence, broken by a few murmurs of "Steady on there," and "Bad form, Charles."

"Bad form?" queried the marquess, his voice ringing along the table. "Lady Margery became engaged to three of my friends and then sent a lying notice to the *Gazette* that it was all a mistake. She did, in fact, through greed and avarice, promise to marry each of the three wealthy young men in the hope of taking the first poor fish who rose to the bait.

"The result, my friends, is that one dueled with the other and nigh lost his life."

Brummell's light, amused voice cut the marquess short. "Really, Charles, your moralistic commendations would be better suited to the Haymarket than to Carlton House."

There was a murmur of assent but the damage had been done. Everyone began to talk at once, carefully looking away from Lady Margery, with the exception of the Prince Regent, who stared at her curiously and then demanded in a loud petulant voice of his neighbors whether what Edgecombe said was true or not.

Hot tears of shame began to roll down

Margery's little nose onto her plate. The more she tried to check them the faster they fell. She had been living in a fool's paradise. Freddie or Toby nearly dead and all because of her. Mr. Moore had turned his shoulder to her and was chattering away as hard as he could to the lady on his other side. There was no way in which Margery could flee the banquet before the Prince Regent decided to take his leave.

Margery cried steadily and painfully as the most magnificent dishes she had ever seen passed and repassed in front of her. She drank her wine feverishly until she finally reached a numbed, dizzied state in which the banquet and its guests seemed very, very small and far away, as if she were looking at everything through the wrong end of a telescope.

The hours of the night dragged on and on, and as the guests consumed more and more wine, several began to look boldly at Lady Margery and make loud comments on her dress, her appearance, and her possible, if doubtful, physical attractions. Mercifully for Margery, by that time her mind had fled to the country of the unhappy drunk, and not one of the jeers or cutting remarks penetrated her befogged brain.

The Marquess of Edgecombe had drunk much more than he normally did. He had planned to revenge his friends. He had dis-

138

graced Lady Margery in the cruelest and most public way he could think of. But he felt neither triumphant nor happy. He felt as if there was a great cloud of guilt lurking somewhere on the horizon of his mind and drank steadily and flirted recklessly to keep it at bay. Lady Margery was on the same side of the table as himself, so he had not seen how she had taken his speech. Probably doesn't give a damn, he reassured himself. Probably getting the two gentlemen next to her to call me out.

At long last the ordeal was over. The prince rose unsteadily to retire. After that, the guests quickly gathered into chattering groups and then took their leave while the servants carried off those too drunk to move themselves. Lady Margery sat bolt upright in front of her plate, a social smile pasted on her face like a rictus.

Mrs. Worthey had fled to her own home without coming in search of Margery. The scandal had quickly spread to the guests in the garden, and Mrs. Worthey had fled from the contamination of such an unfashionable character as Lady Margery.

The resplendent figure of the marquess stood swaying slightly at the entrance to the conservatory. He clutched at one of the gold curtains for support and gazed down the long length to the diminutive figure sitting alone before an untouched plate of food.

The sight sobered him. He marched forward and touched her shoulder. "Come, Lady Margery, it is time to go home," he said.

"Thank you, my lord. Very good, my lord," said Margery, with that hideous smile still fixed on her face.

"I have driven her mad," thought the marquess for a wild moment of panic. Then he realized she was extremely drunk. He put a strong arm round her shoulder and helped her to her feet. "Thank you, my lord. How very kind, my lord," said Lady Margery, and, still supported by his arm, she bowed and curtsied her way down the length of the conservatory thanking innumerable Hanoverian ghosts for a delightful evening.

Chapter Eight

Charles, Marquess of Edgecombe, strode into the smoke-filled gloom of White's in St. James's and immediately saw his three friends sitting in a corner with their heads together.

They were so engrossed in their conversation that they did not hear him approach. Freddie had his arm in a sling made from a blue silk scarf embroidered with gold fleurs-de-lys.

"Hey! Freddie!" said the marquess, slapping him on the back. He then fingered the sling with one polished fingernail. "What is this? Honoring the Bourbons' visit?"

Freddie started like the pale ghost at flash of day and winced. "Oh, it's you, Charles," he said lugubriously. The other two fell silent.

"What's up?" queried the marquess sympathetically. "Liver bad?"

"Could be that, could well be," said Freddie gloomily. "M'liver feels like that Greek fellow's . . . you know, the one tied up on the mountain and two great demned birds are a-peckin' at his liver."

"Prometheus," said the marquess, smiling

faintly. "Didn't know you were bookish, Freddie!"

"Me!" exclaimed Freddie in genuine alarm. "Don't go around saying things like that, Charles. It's just that some of that rot we got at school sticks in m'mind."

"Really," commented the marquess, lowering himself into a chair. "I would have thought they would have successfully eradicated all that from your brain at Oxford."

"They tried," said Freddie seriously.

"Tell him what we was talking about," said Toby suddenly.

"You tell him," said Freddie sulkily. He stroked the silk of his sling. "I ain't well. The doctor said so. Said I was to keep clear of annoyances and alarms. Told my mother so. Yes, he did. Said it plain as day. Said —"

"Oh, shut up!" snapped Viscount Swanley rudely. "It was only a flesh wound and you weren't at death's door for one minute, despite what the Honorable Marquess of Edgecombe cares to shout around the conservatory of Carlton House." He suddenly blushed and stared at his glass.

"Do go on," said the marquess in a silky voice. "You begin to interest me. Some minx makes a fool out of the three of you and yet you censure *my* behavior!"

"Know Yeats-Bartholomew?" asked Toby abruptly.

The marquess raised his thin eyebrows. "Of

course I know him. What has that to do with it?"

"Well," said Toby heavily, "Yeats-Bartholomew's home down in Surrey was about to go under the hammer. Been in the family since they was running around in nothing but woad. So what does he do?" Here he paused dramatically.

"I haven't the faintest idea," drawled the marquess, his heavy lids half closed in a sudden access of boredom.

Toby spoke slowly and distinctly. "He goes and marries that Friday-faced little heiress of a cit, Belinda Josephs. The old home is saved, the repairs done for the first time in a century, everybody happy."

"Splendid!" said the marquess, stifling a yawn.

Three angry pairs of eyes bored into him. "Doesn't it sound familiar?" demanded Toby.

The marquess opened his eyes and straightened up. "Will you all stop talking in riddles and tell me straight whatever it is you are trying, in — may I remark — an extremely convolvuluted way, to tell me."

Freddie, who had been counting the gold fleurs-de-lys on his scarf, raised his head. "I'll tell you," he said.

"The Earl of Chelmswood's back in town, see? He hears a lot of scandalous gossip about Lady Margery. 'Demme,' he roars out in the middle of Chitworth's breakfast yesterday, 'Thought m'daughter didn't want another season. Berkeley Square, did y'say? Must be someone else. Margery hasn't money enough for a season on her own, let alone a town house.'

"Well, the countess, she looks round the room with eyes like carriage lamps turning a corner, and first thing she wants to know is whether Lady Margery was wearing a great diamond-and-ruby necklace when last seen. Everyone says, 'No.' 'Aha!' she screams, 'she sold *my* necklace!' ' 'Tain't your necklace,' says the earl.

"The countess screams she wants it, on and on — dashed embarrassing it was — and the earl says he'll find who Margery sold it to and buy it back. 'What with?' says the countess, and I tell you, Charles, the acid in her voice made me shiver. So the earl starts to mumble and the countess lowers her voice too — but not enough, y'know. We all heard her *demanding* that the earl sell Chelmswood immediately, and it seems as if Lady Margery's to live with that horror Desdemona as an unpaid companion.

"We all got to thinkin'. Heard about Yeats-Bartholomew and thought again. Nobody called him a minx. Nobody insults him in front of the Prince Regent. Hard on Margery, don't you see?" And Freddie collapsed, exhausted, after the longest speech of his life.

The marquess opened his mouth and

snapped it shut again. He was haunted by a picture of Margery as he had last seen her. She had still had that awful smile on her face as he had delivered her into the arms of her butler. But she was a *woman,* dammit! It was all right for a man to go to any lengths to save his ancestral home. But a woman should confine her activities to her watercolor box, some knowledge of the globes and the pianoforte, and the pleasant science of how to charm a man.

And she had said herself that Chelmswood was only bricks and mortar, after all. Perhaps his friends had exaggerated the new countess's character. Perhaps Desdemona would make Margery happy and guide her to a suitable marriage.

"What were you thinking of doing about it?" he asked his friends.

"We-e-ll," said Viscount Swanley slowly. "We were thinking of giving her some money, enough to keep the wolves at bay . . . and . . ."

"And the earl would probably dissipate it in a couple of weeks of drinking and gambling," said the marquess. "You must not forget the heartless way that —"

"You behaved," put in Toby suddenly. "No need to cut up at her in front of Prinny that way."

The marquess looked thoughtfully at three pairs of accusing eyes. He could hardly explain to himself why he had been so unkind at the Prince Regent's banquet. But when he had seen her entering the room looking so small and frail and childlike, it had somehow driven him into an unaccustomed fury.

The marquess was perhaps his own severest critic.

"I shall call on the earl," he said, rising to his feet. "I shall probably find that your worries are groundless and that there is no cause to be concerned about Lady Margery Quennell!"

With that, he walked from the club with long athletic strides, leaving his friends to stare after him in amazement.

The marquess was ushered into the magnificent Egyptian saloon at the Earl's town house in Grosvenor Square. Austere gold-and-black wallpaper complemented the backless sofas and the glass sphynxes' heads winking from the pilasters of the fireplace. A black carpet with a gold Egyptian border spread luxuriously across the room, which had been designed with an eye to fashion rather than to taste, for the chairs, with their huge ball-and-claw feet, were upholstered in black and white stripes, garish and shocking to the eye.

Desdemona, Countess of Chelmswood, rose from one of these chairs and floated forward to meet him, emerging from the barred furniture like an aristocrat escaping from the Bastille.

She was a vision of loveliness in gold tissue, which was cunningly damped to show all the charms of a breathtaking figure. Her hair was like spun gold and her eyes as blue as the marquess's own. Her smile was particularly sweet and welcoming, and the marquess felt a great cloud of guilt and worry lift from his brow. An angel such as this would surely take good care of Margery.

He introduced himself. In a soft little voice, the countess explained that the earl would join them presently.

She began to entertain him prettily with a fund of surprisingly antique gossip. The marquess felt encouraged to broach the problem of Margery.

Desdemona gave a trilling laugh. My lord must not be concerned over his behavior at Carlton House. Margery had behaved like the veriest romp and was in need of a set-down. It would do her the world of good.

The marquess blinked. But it was all said so prettily and with such genuine concern. However, he felt tempted to pursue the subject, and would have done so, had not the earl walked into the room.

He seemed to have grown much older than when the marquess had seen him last. Purple veins throbbed on his red face and his large hands trembled ever so slightly under a fall of exquisite Mechlin lace.

"Good to see you, Charles," roared the earl. "I trust my bride has been keeping you well entertained."

Was there a flicker of suspicion in the earl's red-veined eye, or had it been a trick of the light? Before the marquess could answer, the countess cast down her eyes and her mouth formed itself into a little Mona Lisa smile. The earl stared at her, his hands twitching the more, and the marquess realized to his horror that with every look and gesture the countess was implying all sorts of intrigues and attractions between herself and the marquess.

"Well, what can I do for you?" asked the earl in a flat voice.

"I am interested in the welfare of Lady Margery . . ." began the marquess, and fell back slightly before the pure glare of venom on the countess's face.

"I saw the necklace — Margery's necklace — in Rundell and Bridge," said Desdemona. "See how she insults you, Jimmy. Your family heirloom there for all the world to see! You must buy it back!"

"Look, Des," pleaded the earl, writhing in embarrassment. "Not at all the thing, got company, you know. Dear me, what you must think of my mischievous little puss, Charles."

As if to illustrate his words, the mischievous little puss curled her long pointed nails into claws.

"Anyway," went on the earl, in a mock jovial tone and throwing a nervous look at his fulminating wife, "Margery's back at Chelmswood and very well by all accounts. 'Course, you may have heard, I will need to sell the old place. But my Des will look after Margery. Find her a husband, heh!"

"If that is possible," replied Desdemona sweetly. "But she must curb that arrogant manner first. As my companion, I expect to be *obeyed*. How will she learn to obey a husband if she not learn to obey me?"

"But surely," protested the marquess with some vigor, "your own daughter, sir, would be an honored guest in your household. It is unheard of, surely, to have your own daughter working as a companion to your wife!"

"Who *are* you to come and preach to us," hissed Desdemona suddenly. "Why this great interest in Margery? If you are so concerned with her welfare, my fine lord, I suggest you marry her and take her off our hands."

It was then that the Marquess of Edgecombe surprised the earl and countess and surprised himself.

He leaned his broad shoulders against the mantelpiece, folded his arms, and surveyed the earl and Desdemona with contempt.

"Marry Lady. Margery!" he repeated. "Marry Margery? As a matter of fact, my lady, that is precisely what I will do, and I will also take Chelmswood off your hands and give it to Lady Margery as a wedding present!"

"It's no use," said Lady Margery Quennell miserably. "No one will marry me now."

Lady Amelia looked at her young friend and shook her head sadly. After such a monumental humiliation as the episode at Carlton House, no young lady could hope any longer for marriage. A few people had been surprisingly kind, and even Mr. George Brummell had sent Margery a charming letter full of nonsense and gossip. Amelia blamed herself more than Margery. She, Amelia, was the older and therefore should surely have been the wiser. She knew Chuffley was miserable about the state of affairs as well.

The full glory of a perfect summer's day blazed round Chelmswood, sparkling like diamonds in the mullioned windows and bringing a lazy, sleepy hush to the great park, but all Margery could notice was how each sunbeam picked out the bare patches in the carpet and mercilessly highlighted the stained and worn upholstery.

Both women were engaged in darning linen sheets.

"But he escorted you home," said Amelia suddenly.

There was no need for Margery to ask who

she meant by "he."

"He was very drunk, I believe," said Margery coldly, stabbing her needle into the linen as if it were the marquess's heart.

"So were you," said Amelia fretfully, and then laid down her own needle and burst into tears. "I c-can't bear it," she sobbed. "I can't bear to s-see you looking so *old* and worn."

Margery stared at her shocked. She had never seen her placid friend cry before. She felt a great rush of shame. She had been brooding on her own troubles and forgetting all the while of the bleak future that also faced her old friend.

Margery threw aside the linen and rushed across the room to embrace her friend, whose shoulders were still heaving with the violence of her sobs.

"There, there, Amelia! What a selfish beast I am! Quietly, now. Quietly. We are fretting ourselves to flinders over what may never happen. Why! Papa may decide yet not to sell Chelmswood from under us."

"Mr. Jessieman," announced Chuffley in accents of doom.

The small figure of the earl's man of business edged itself apologetically into the room. Distractedly Amelia dried her eyes on one of the sheets and then bustled off to supervise the making of tea.

Margery pressed her small spine firmly

against the back of the chair and said in a flat voice, "What news do you bring?"

Mr. Jessieman sat down nervously on a chair opposite and addressed the empty fireplace.

"The earl has informed me that he has sold Chelmswood. He would not name the buyer but would only say that the gentleman who is buying Chelmswood will call today."

He turned his eyes at last to Margery's white face and said with unwonted violence:

"This does not please me . . . does not please me at all! The earl's manner was cocky to say the least. I have been forced to the conclusion that he cares for nought but cards, drink, and his countess. Forgive me for being so bold, my lady. I am overwrought."

"The countess must be looking forward to my company," said Margery through stiff lips.

Mr. Jessieman scratched his head under his wig. "Well, there's the puzzle," he said. "The countess was not pleased, but it seemed almost as if she envied you. 'Margery does not deserve such good fortune,' she said."

"Sarcasm," commented Margery bluntly.

"Far from it, my lady," said Mr. Jessieman. "The countess appeared . . . well, *jealous*."

"Then she is a fool," snapped Margery. "Damn these mushrooms who care neither for land or heritage!"

"The countess comes from a very old family," suggested Mr. Jessieman timidly.

"Pah!" Margery rose to her feet and began to pace the room. "Blood means nothing. There is more good breeding in one of my stable lads than there is in the Countess of Chelmswood."

Mr. Jessieman reflected that this was probably true, since a large number of the staff bore a remarkable resemblance to the earl, but did not consider it politic to mention the fact.

Amelia came in with the tea tray and was quickly apprised of their fate. Chuffley passed round the tea things, his expression like wood.

After drinking his tea in worried silence, Mr. Jessieman retired to his rooms, leaving Amelia and Margery alone.

"It is almost a relief now that the blow has fallen," said Margery slowly. "I wonder who has bought Chelmswood."

The doorbell clanged loudly and both women jumped.

"That will be our answer," said Margery, getting to her feet.

There was the sound of an altercation in the hallway and then the door burst open. The Marquess of Edgecombe stood staring into the room.

"I tried to refuse him, my lady," shouted Chuffley over the marquess's broad shoulder, "but he pushed his way in."

"How dare you, sir!" stormed Margery.

"I dare because I have your father's permission," said the marquess with a sweet smile. He sat down uninvited and stretched his long legs, encased in a pair of gleaming Hessians, out in front of him.

"You see," he added, "*I* have bought Chelmswood."

Chapter Nine

"*You!*" said Lady Margery Quennell in a voice of loathing. "I might have known. Could you not have waited until we had left, my lord? Needs must you come to gloat?"

"Oh, I didn't come to gloat," he said laconically, flicking a speck of dust from one of his boots. "I have a proposition to put to you, Lady Margery . . . in private."

He got to his feet and walked to the door, looking at Amelia and pointedly holding it open. Amelia looked from Margery to the marquess in bewilderment, but Margery gave a slight nod of dismissal and Amelia dropped a curtsy, which was more like a stagger, and left.

The marquess slammed the door behind her and rested his shoulders against it.

Margery clasped her trembling hands and summoned up her courage. "What is your proposition, my lord?"

"Marriage," he said bluntly.

She looked at him in stunned silence. He seemed very sober.

"That is what you wished, Lady Margery, is it not?" went on the marquess with infuriating calm. "Marriage in return for the safety of your home?"

"I c-can only gather that you are funning," said Margery. "Did you not have enough revenge at Carlton House?"

His thin face flushed. "This proposal of marriage is by way of making amends for my behavior, Lady Margery. You yourself are not entirely blameless, you know."

"Indeed, I must have been mad," admitted Margery, raising her small hands to her hot cheeks. "But it was cruel to let me believe that Freddie was at death's door. I suffered agony until my servants reported to me that he had suffered no more than a flesh wound. But you have had your revenge. I have been left with neither character or home."

"I am offering you a way to regain both," he pointed out. "Come, Lady Margery, you do not appear to be lacking in common sense. There is not only yourself to think of you know.

"You must think also of the future of your servants . . . and of Lady Amelia."

"Where should we live if we were married?" asked Margery, wondering why she should even entertain the thought of marriage to this terrifying rake.

He gave her an enigmatic look from under heavy lids. "You may live here . . . for a time . . . until you become used to the idea."

Margery's ever-optimistic mind did not

hear the "for a time" and grasped at the rest.

"You mean, I could stay at Chelmswood? With Lady Amelia?"

"But not indefinitely," he murmured. "You will be my wife, you know."

Margery looked at him quickly. He seemed so remote, his eyes betraying only polite interest. She *had* heard of many marriages where the couples seemed to suit themselves.

"If it makes it easier for you," he said. "I wish a wife, and you, my dear . . . er . . . wish Chelmswood."

It all seemed so beautifully simple. Margery gazed round at her beloved home. The threadbare patches seemed to vanish from the carpets and the worn stains from the upholstery.

"A marriage of convenience," she cried.

The marquess made a slight bow. "If it pleases you to call it that."

There had been a note of mockery in his voice, and Margery looked into his eyes. But his face was a polite mask.

He watched with quiet amusement the different emotions chasing each other across Margery's mobile little face. Margery was convincing herself as hard and fast as she could that this was an answer to her prayers. He would surely . . . he had indicated . . . that she need not expect any intimacy from the marriage. Amelia would be safe. And Chuffley. And the rest of the old servants.

She took a deep breath.

"Very well, my lord. I accept."

The marquess moved towards her and Margery nervously took a step back. But he only raised one little hand to his lips.

"You have made me very happy, Margery," he said, releasing her hand and gazing down at her. Her face was very pale, he noted, and she had lost a great deal of weight. Her tiny figure seemed as frail and delicate as porcelain. He was seized with a sudden rush of tenderness for her. He wanted to draw her onto his knee and comfort her. Instead he asked, "I trust a wedding in two days' time would not be too rushed?"

"S-so soon," faltered Margery.

"We have no reason to wait," he pointed out. "We can be married by special license. Your father in all probability will have returned to Paris. My father is in poor health and avoids social occasions. Come! Say 'yes.' Think how joyful the servants will be."

"Oh, very well," muttered Margery ungraciously. He looked down at her with some amusement.

"May I also suggest that we pretend that this is a love match? You surely do not wish to distress anyone by letting them think you are sacrificing yourself."

"Do you mean I have to . . . to . . . *kiss* you in front of people?" asked Margery, horrified.

"It will be sufficient if you hold my hand," he said calmly. "Now, call them in and get it over with."

Margery rang the bell. Chuffley appeared with suspicious promptitude. The marquess was sure he had been leaning against the door outside. His old face was wreathed in smiles.

Margery was assailed with a sudden feeling of unreality. The marquess had moved over to stand beside her and was encircling her shoulders with a strong arm. She forced herself to smile up at him.

"Bring everyone here, Chuffley. I have good news for you all," she said.

Amelia was the first to arrive, looking breathless and worried, then Mr. Jessieman, bleary and sleepy, and then the upper servants. Margery opened her mouth and emitted a strangled squeak and looked wildly at the marquess for help.

The marquess felt her thin shoulders trembling beneath his arm and gave her a reassuring squeeze.

"I have the honor," he said, addressing the curious crowd, "to announce my forthcoming betrothal to Lady Margery."

There was a stunned silence and then a tremendous crash. Lady Amelia had fainted dead away.

For the next forty-eight hours the marquess

swept all before him with ruthless efficiency. The special license was procured, the wedding was to take place in the Chelmswood church, and a squad of workmen were employed to transform a dusty suite of rooms in the deserted east wing into a bridal suite. Margery and Amelia spent the time in a frenzy of sewing, transforming Margery's mother's wedding dress into a more fashionable line. It was heavily encrusted with gold and seed pearls which had an irritating habit of escaping from their threads and rolling under the furniture.

Amelia had just recovered what she felt to be the thousandth, her back was aching, and her head was in a whirl. The first shock of surprise had gone, leaving her worried and anxious about her young niece. Margery had been strangely quiet and withdrawn, only occasionally rousing herself to parry Amelia's curious questions. When had Margery first realized that she was in love with the marquess? Margery could not say. Would they eventually be moving to the marquess's home? Margery had no idea. Amelia had delicately asked if Margery had planned to order new nightclothes, and Margery had snapped, "Oh, any old thing will do," and when Amelia had shown her surprise, Margery had muttered something incoherent and fled from the room.

Margery could not understand her own

feelings. Every time she saw him, the marquess looked more disturbingly attractive than ever. He was extremely affectionate in public and cold and withdrawn on the few short occasions when they were in private together.

But she would have gone to the altar hoping he were a little in love with her were it not for the unexpected arrival of the earl and the countess, complete with retinue of servants, on the day before the wedding.

The earl was looking remarkably shamefaced and said that "his little puss" had pointed out to him that he was behaving like an unnatural father in avoiding his only daughter's wedding.

Margery privately thought it would have been more natural as far as her father was concerned to avoid the whole thing, not favoring any occasion where he could not roll the dice or hold a hand at cards. They planned to leave after the wedding breakfast, and Margery settled herself to endure their short visit.

The earl and the countess retired to their rooms before dinner, and Margery retired to hers in the hope of catching some much-needed rest. Her looking glass told her that she was rapidly degenerating into the Margery of old, and no amount of dressing or paint could disguise the strain in her eyes or the hollows in her cheeks.

As it turned out, she was not fated to be left alone for long. There was a slight scratching on the door and then, without waiting for a reply, Desdemona sailed into the room, resplendent in paper-thin Indian muslin that left little of her charms to the imagination.

She tiptoed forward and wound her arms round Margery's neck and deposited a moist kiss on her cheek. "My poor, poor girl," she sighed.

Margery turned away from her and began to brush her hair vigorously, "Indeed, I am more to be congratulated than pitied," snapped Margery.

"Poor innocent," murmured Desdemona. "I have been talking to your father, *dear* — now please turn to me and attend — and although we are happy that you are marrying a fortune, we feel you are rather like a little baa-lamb being led to the slaughter."

"Fiddle," said Lady Margery.

The countess gave a pretty sigh. "Oh, I see you have not the faintest idea of what I am talking about." She leaned forward. "Tell me, dear Margery, do you know aught of the relations between a man and a woman?"

Margery put down the hairbrush and surveyed her slowly. She was aware of a multitude of mixed emotions: fury with Desdemona for her impertinence; visions of animals coupling in the fields; and memories of the marquess's reputation.

"Please leave," she said finally. "I shall manage very well without any advice from you, Desdemona."

Desdemona's eyes narrowed angrily. "Then I shall not try to help you, you ungrateful drab." And before Margery could guess her intent, Desdemona had seized her by the shoulders and twisted her round so that she was facing the looking glass.

"Look at yourself!" hissed Desdemona. "And think . . . think *why* the notorious Marquess of Edgecombe should wish to have *you* in his bed."

Margery looked miserably from her own careworn face to the glowing if vicious one of Desdemona.

"I will tell you why," said Desdemona, her long nails digging through the thin material of Margery's dress. "It is because our notorious rake has a soft place in his heart for lame ducks. And you, my dear, are *very* lame. Notice that hound he always has with him when he goes out riding? Not a distinguished animal, you must admit. He found it being beaten to death in a London gutter. But it was not enough for the marquess to put the beast in his stables. He needs must make it his favorite hound and take it with him everywhere. Poor Margery. A little pet mongrel, that is all you are!"

Margery stared at her dressing table. The

sunlight filtering through the lace curtains of her bedroom window flickered across the bottles of scents and lotions. There was a large bottle of patchouli, a scent Margery particularly loathed, lying unopened. With one deft movement, she twisted off the top and poured the contents over Desdemona's immaculately coiffed head.

"Take that," blazed Margery. " 'Tis a scent for strumpets and it becomes you well!"

Desdemona's nails flashed out and clawed at Margery's cheek, and then she burst into noisy tears and ran from the room.

Margery sat for a long time as if turned to stone, a thin trickle of blood dripping from her scratched face and falling unheeded onto her dress.

There was a clatter of hoofs in the driveway below, and, walking like a martinet, she crossed to the window and pushed open the lattice.

The marquess was dismounting from his horse. A shaggy, lolloping mongrel with enormous paws danced round and round him, panting in adoration. The marquess smiled and stooped down and scratched the dog behind the ears and the animal looked up at him with its heart in its eyes.

"I shall not become like that," thought Margery, backing from the window. The poison of Desdemona's words had dripped into her soul. She had begun to wildly hope that the elegant marquess had indeed formed a *tendre* for her.

He had said he was trying to atone for his behavior at Carlton House and she had not really listened to him, having a certain amount of natural feminine vanity. Had Desdemona not mentioned that wretched dog, then Margery would have believed her to be merely jealous. It was too late to cancel the marriage. The servants were singing about their work and Amelia was once more the plump and happy matron she used to be. She must go through with it.

The marquess looked across the drawing room that evening at the spectacle presented by his bride, with some irritation. There was no denying that her hair and dress were all the crack, but her face and manner were colorless and she hardly spoke. In contrast, Desdemona chattered and flirted and giggled and ogled. The earl was slumped in a wing chair, not quite drunk and not quite sober, gazing with doglike adoration at the countess, and Margery shuddered. He looked remarkably like the marquess's dog.

The marquess was impeccable in black and white evening dress. A sapphire stickpin winkèd in his cravat, matching the intense blue of his eyes. He suddenly crossed to Margery's side and put an arm round her shoulders. She cringed at his touch and his brows snapped together in irritation. He was about to ask her what on earth was the matter when the supper bell was rung and everyone started filing towards the dining room.

The marquess was seated on Margery's right and he set himself to please. Nothing could have been more loverlike than his various attentions, and nothing, Margery reflected, could have been harder than the expression in his eyes.

The marquess was beginning to suffer from an extreme bout of premarital nerves. He looked at his drab and silent fiancée, at her father, who was now definitely bosky, and at the beautiful and empty face of the countess. He had a longing to run from the dining room, jump on his horse, and ride and ride as far and as fast from Chelmswood as possible.

The interminable evening came to an end at last. Lady Margery cried herself to sleep and the marquess dreamed long and horrible dreams of life imprisonment.

Lady Margery descended the ancient oaken stair of Chelmswood, feeling very strange and quite unlike herself. There is undoubtedly some good fairy who looks after brides on their wedding day. Although Margery could hardly be called radiant, there was a translucent glow on her pale face, and the dress, heavily encrusted with gold and pearls, gave her small figure a regal air.

Her father began to cry great sentimental tears — "one part salt and two parts old wine," thought Margery cynically. He was also sweating profusely, from alcohol, nerves, and remorse.

"Are you sure you ain't throwin' yourself away?" bleated the earl, mopping the accumulation of liquid from his face with a large handkerchief.

"Yes, yes!" said Margery testily. "Let's get on with it!"

"See how anxious our bride is!" tittered Desdemona. "You're a bit late to be worrying about it now, Jimmy."

The earl turned on her in a sudden fury. "You're *common*, Des, that's what you are. Never told you before. Common as dirt!"

Desdemona let out a hiss of pure rage. "And you're a drunken old fool. D'you think it's *fun* for me to share your bed — to have that great body — ?"

Amelia let out a squawk of alarm and threw herself between the earl and countess. "You will please curb your arguments on Margery's wedding day," she said in her haughtiest voice. "James! Take Margery's arm to the carriage, and you" — here she gave Desdemona a hard stare — "will follow with me."

The sun blazed down on a perfect day.

The earl was mercifully silent on the road to the church.

Chelmswood Church dated back to Norman times, with a squat square tower and a pleasant shaggy churchyard where the gravestones stood at lopsided angles and every bird in England seemed to gather to sing.

Margery breathed in the familiar Anglican smell of wood smoke, damp prayer books, dry rot, and incense and felt a great calm descending on her. The village organist was murdering Bach as he had done on all the Sundays stretching back to her baptism. The familiar faces of her tenants smiled at her out of the gloom, and the only unfamiliar things were the tall figure of the marquess standing at the altar and that of his best man — no other than Freddie Jamieson.

The service passed as if in a dream. Some other Margery seemed to be making the responses. Then the marquess stooped to kiss her and she felt his lips cool and impersonal against her own.

Then out into the sunshine again under the swinging clamor of the bells and surrounded by the cheers and cries of the villagers.

The wedding breakfast, to which most of the local county had been asked, was laid out on long tables on the lawns in front of Chelmswood.

Margery smiled and bowed and listened to the toasts and drank a considerable amount of iced champagne, feeling all the while that the old house was tying her to her childhood and that the familiar setting was stopping her from realizing that she was in fact married to one of the handsomest and richest men in England.

The twilight deepened, and one by one the guests began to leave. The marquess did not wish any rowdy revels outside his bedroom windows on his wedding night.

He looked down at his bride. She was talking to Freddie on her other side and showing more animation than she had done all day.

Suddenly it was dark and Amelia was whispering in her ear that it was time to retire and followed by a vindictive titter from Desdemona, Margery went slowly indoors. She had drunk too much and eaten too little. She seemed to float up the great dark staircase and along the twisting corridors that led to the east wing. She paused with Amelia outside her new bedroom door, realizing in a fuzzy way that she had not inspected her new quarters, having left all the arrangements to the marquess.

She pushed open the door and went in.

A footman followed behind them and busily moved about the room lighting great branches of candles.

Amelia looked timidly round. "It is perhaps a rather *masculine* room, Margery. But no doubt you will wish to make some changes when you settle down."

A great four-poster bed draped in heavy crimson silk dominated the room. A fine tapestry of a particularly brutal hunting scene decorated one wall and the rest were hung with heavy, dark flock wallpaper and embellished with hunting scenes in ornate gilt frames.

Margery looked around her vaguely. "It will do," she said indifferently, and received a surprised and anxious look from Amelia. Battersby bustled into the room and set about getting her mistress ready for bed, turning the unresisting Margery this way and that as if she were a rag doll.

Finally Margery was left alone to wait for her lord.

The room seemed uncomfortably bright, so she snuffed most of the candles with the exception of one branch over the fireplace. The summer breeze blew in from the garden, bringing with it the smell of sweet-smelling stock, roses, and freshly cut grass. Margery wandered aimlessly about the room, picking things up and putting them down. A door beside the tapestry led to a small dressing room. There was a narrow bed over in the corner by the window and Margery's heart leapt with relief at the sight of it. Perhaps he did not mean to sleep with her after all. Hard on the heels of that emotion came an irrational feeling of defeat. The marquess must have had love affairs with many beauties. He would probably not feel himself honor-bound to consummate a mere marriage of convenience — until he decided he wanted an heir.

The effects of the champagne were slowly dissipating and she felt very young and forlorn. She climbed up into the great bed, closed her eyes, and waited patiently for sleep.

The sound of the door opening made her sit up with a gasp. She had finally convinced herself that the marquess would not come and was shocked to see him standing in the doorway of his dressing room wrapped in an elaborate dressing gown embroidered in blue and gold. Without looking at her, he walked across and snuffed out the candles. She heard the whisper of silk as he removed his dressing gown, and pressed herself back against the pillows.

"Is this necessary, my lord?" whispered Margery.

"Very necessary," came the mocking reply from somewhere in the darkness. "And my name is Charles."

Margery sensed a great bulk looming over her in the darkness. "Charles," she cried in a pleading voice.

He was in bed beside her. He was drawing her closer.

"Now, madame wife," said the Marquess of Edgecombe, "come here to me!"

Chapter Ten

The Marquess of Edgecombe twisted round in bed and stared down at the face of his sleeping wife. He was shocked, puzzled, and worried.

He knew that many country-bred girls like Margery who went in for strenuous sports such as hunting did not come to their marriage bed *virgo intacto*.

But nonetheless, he was troubled. Instead of the shy, frightened girl who would have to be coaxed in the arts of lovemaking, he had found himself in the arms of a fiery, sensuous woman who had returned passion for passion until *he* had been left trembling and shaking and feeling like a novice.

The trick she had played on his three friends, which had recently seemed the desperate move of an innocent girl determined to save her home, now appeared as if it might have been the ploy of an experienced woman. He knew very little about Margery Quennell. His amours had always been with experienced women of the demimonde. And that was why these women existed. It was downright *indecent* for any gently bred girl to behave with the abandon that his wife had shown.

He looked down at his wife again. Her face looked very young and innocent. He traced the faint scratches on her cheek and wondered again where she had got them.

She stirred in her sleep at his touch and then opened her eyes and looked straight up at him. She stretched like a cat and murmured something and then wound her arms round his neck.

Her slim body seemed to throb and pulsate against him, and the marquess's last coherent thought before he was carried away on a tide of passion was, "Dammit, she might at least have *blushed*."

It was Margery's turn to awaken first. The sun was high in the sky and her lord was asleep. She propped herself up on one elbow and gazed at him tenderly. He loved her after all!

She looked lazily around the room and judged that the other door must lead to her own dressing room. Stiff and sore, she climbed down from the bed and made her way on trembling legs across the floor. She looked back at the sleeping marquess and had a sudden longing to climb back into that large, beautiful bed and fall asleep on his shoulder. But she was anxious to look her best for him when he awoke, so instead she moved into her dressing room, noting with amusement that it was as masculine as her lord's, and rang for Battersby. Half an hour later, she tripped lightly down the stairs to find the Honorable Freddie helping himself liberally to breakfast.

Freddie looked at her glowing face and the last of his doubts about Margery fled. "Morning!" he hailed cheerfully. "Been looking round your place and I must say I don't blame you a bit for fighting hard to keep it. Would do the same thing meself."

"Oh, Freddie," said Margery mistily, "you are a very *generous* young man."

"Ain't I just," grinned Freddie, "and Toby and Perry send their regards too."

Both ate their breakfast in companionable silence and then Margery volunteered to show Freddie the grounds.

"This is just like old times," said Freddie enthusiastically. "You're the only female I ever met who didn't make me feel awkward. Wish you happy, Margery."

"I *am* happy," cried Margery. She stood on tiptoe to give him a sisterly kiss on the cheek. At the same time, Freddie turned his head in surprise and received the kiss full on his mouth.

"Oh, Freddie! How *fast* you must think me!" cried Margery.

"Don't think of it," said Freddie cheerfully, tucking her hand in his arm. "Supposed to kiss the bride anyway, you know."

The marquess let the curtain drop. He had been fooled like a regular greenhorn. She had walked straight from his arms into Freddie's. No need to call Freddie out. That passionate kiss had been entirely Margery's idea.

Then if she wanted marriage *à la mode* she should have it. Two could play at that game. He pulled savagely at the bell rope and gave his surprised valet orders to pack.

Margery and Freddie turned at the end of the long drive and made their way leisurely back to the house. The tall Tudor chimneys of Chelmswood rose above the trees, which whispered in the lightest of summer breezes. There was no worry or care left in the world for Margery.

Then she and Freddie drew back hurriedly to the side of the drive as a traveling carriage pulled by four matched bays came hurtling down the drive towards them. As it swept past, they were afforded a fleeting glimpse of the Marquess of Edgecombe's excellent profile.

Margery looked at her companion in dismay. "Why didn't he stop, Freddie? Where can he be going?"

"Must be something up with his father," said Freddie anxiously.

They hurried towards the house. Chuffley was waiting for them with an unreadable expression on his face. He mutely held out a small silver tray bearing a long letter. With trembling fingers, Margery tore it open.

Its message was brief.

"Madam," the marquess had written. "Since you have obviously gained what you wanted from this marriage and your wants do not include me, I trust you will enjoy your first love — your home — and your second loves, of which you obviously have many.

"I am determined, however, that we present a respectable front to the *ton*. I shall expect you to join me at my town house for the start of the Little Season."

It was coldly signed "Edgecombe."

Margery stood reading it over and over again. What had made him so angry? What had she done?

She suddenly recalled her passionate love-making of the night before and felt ready to sink with shame. What had seemed so natural and so beautiful to her must have seemed an everyday occurrence to such an experienced man. Her inexperienced love-making must have seemed gauche and tepid.

Her eyes filled with angry tears. What else did he expect from an inexperienced girl? He had not given her a chance to prove her love. The cold letter was like a slap in the face. Never again should he make her tremble with passion. There was no real world outside the covers of a three-volume romance. Love in reality was a charade and marriage a sham.

She and her father were indeed a sorry

pair, both tied to heartless fribbles.

She would join him for the Little Season, and, with the help of Battersby's genius, she would prove to the sneering, heartless, aristocrat who was her husband that there were at least other men who would appreciate her.

The crisp autumn leaves crackled under the curricle wheels as the marquess edged his way through the fashionable press.

It was the fashionable hour in the park when everyone turned out to see or be seen.

"Thought you'd given up all this nonsense," said Toby from his perch beside the marquess. "What are we doing here, anyway?"

"Shopping," said the marquess briefly, his eyes raking over the crowd.

Toby opened his mouth in surprise and then closed it again. He didn't understand his friend one bit. Charles had been deuced odd since his wedding. Never mentioned Margery, and received all congratulations on his marriage as if they were insults.

He came out of his reverie to notice that the marquess had reined in beside a smart-looking landau. The occupant was equally dashing and was smiling up at the marquess in an intimate way that made Toby sigh with envy.

"Mrs. Harrison, I believe," said the marquess, bowing low.

The lady let out a little trill of laughter and opened her pretty little mouth. "La! Ain't you the bold one, my lord," she fluttered, "and us not even introduced."

Toby winced at the vulgar whine of her voice and waited for his friend to give her one of his famous set-downs.

To his horror the marquess said, "Your beauty, madam, is sufficient introduction. But if I have offended you . . ."

"Aw, no," grinned Mrs. Harrison.

"Then perhaps you will do me the inestimable honor of furnishing me with your direction so that I may . . . er . . . call on you."

"I should be delighted," said Mrs. Harrison, giving him an address in Half Moon Street.

"This evening, perhaps?" queried the marquess.

"This evening," confirmed the lady with a languishing flutter of her eyelashes.

"This evening . . . *late?*"

"I keep late hours, my lord," said Mrs. Harrison with a genteel simper, awful to behold.

"I look forward to the delightful charms of your . . . er . . . company," said the marquess in a caressing voice that teetered on the edge of insult.

He bowed and the landau moved off.

"Not a word, Toby," said the marquess savagely. "Not a single word!"

★ ★ ★

When he arrived back at his town house, he was informed of Lady Margery's arrival from the country.

The marquess's lips tightened into a thin line. "Pray be good enough to convey my respects to my lady," he told the servant, "and tell her that I wish to see her *immediately*. I shall be in the library."

The marquess strode into that room and looked around him with distaste. Works of various authors, bought by the yard by his father, lined the walls. His own books lay scattered on occasional tables and in piles on the floor. A long low table covered with magazines and newspapers crouched before the empty fireplace surrounded by massive carved chairs. Like elsewhere in the house, there was no evidence of a feminine touch, and the Marquess felt irrationally that Margery should have done something about it, not pausing to consider that she could hardly be expected to move the furniture around on the day of her arrival.

The door opened and Margery came in, hesitating on the threshold and giving him an inquiring glance. She was wearing a morning dress of heavy green crepe, slim and high waisted, falling to three deep flounces. Her sandy hair was elaborately dressed and gleamed with highlights in the pale autumn sunshine. The marquess felt angrily that she had no right to look so well.

For her part, Margery thought her husband looked distractingly handsome and she gave a little sigh of resignation. How could she have expected anyone so devastating to fall in love with little Margery Quennell?

"Sit down, madam," said the marquess, waving his hand towards one of the repellent chairs.

"Oh call me Margery," said that young lady with a flash of spirit. "I am well aware that you are in a bad temper about something. Perhaps you would now care to tell me what *that* something is?"

The marquess looked at her from under hooded lids. He had not expected such a direct question. How could one possibly tell one's wife that one had doubts about her morals?

"I have realized that it was a mistake to get married," he said cruelly. "I am too used to my bachelor freedom. But I will afford you the same freedom, my lady, provided you are discreet."

Margery flushed with annoyance. "Very well, my lord. Have you anything further to say?"

The marquess put up his quizzing glass and surveyed his wife. She stared back at him, resting her pointed chin on her hand.

"We shall, of course, appear at various functions together," he said coldly, letting the glass fall. "I would not have it broadcast to the world I had made a mistake."

"Have you plans for this evening?" asked Margery, equally coldly.

"I shall be privately engaged," he said, crossing to the window and staring out into the street, with his hand holding the curtain.

"I see," said Margery, staring at his profile while a cold anger slowly took possession of her.

There was a long silence. Outside in the street, a group of strolling acrobats were twisting and tumbling to the squeaky music of a fiddle. One of them saw the marquess watching from the window and executed several handsprings, ending in a low bow. The marquess dropped the curtain and turned back towards the room.

But his wife had gone.

He felt as if he had just lost some battle. Why should he spend the night sampling Mrs. Harrison's doubtful charms if his wife were to know nothing about it? He came to a sudden decision. He would be seen in public with Mrs. Harrison. Not among the *haut ton* but somewhere guaranteed to send a little ripple of discreet gossip running across London in Margery's direction.

Margery sat upstairs in her boudoir. She was too angry for tears. She wanted revenge. She wanted the marquess to know that she,

Margery, was quite capable of enjoying as much bachelor freedom as her husband. She scribbled a note, folded it into a cocked hat, and sent a servant off in search of Mr. Freddie Jamieson.

Chapter Eleven

The walks and boxes of Vauxhall pleasure gardens were crowded to capacity as Margery and Freddie strolled amicably along. They had just attended a stirring performance of "The Battle of Borodino" by Mrs. Salmon under the gilded cockleshell in the center of the gardens and were returning to their box to join Lady Amelia.

"This was *such* a good idea, Freddie," sighed Margery. "I should have felt so alone otherwise."

Freddie bit his lip. He was once again enjoying the novelty of squiring a lady but he had no wish to see the Marquess of Edgecombe's face blazing at him from behind a yard of cold steel.

"Charles all right?" he ventured. "I mean to say, newly married and all that. I mean to say, shouldn't you . . . er . . . Shouldn't he . . ." He thrust the knob of his cane in his mouth like a stopper and let his eyebrows, which were wiggling up to his hairline, ask the questions for him.

"It is a modern marriage, you see," said Margery with a lightness she did not feel.

"Charles does not concern himself with what I do."

Lady Amelia was waiting for them in their box. She had been joined by Toby Sanderson and an equally large man who bore a marked resemblance to Toby.

Toby introduced his elder brother, Archie, Lord Brenton, who gave Margery a stiff bow and a very hard stare from the family hall-mark of bulging green eyes.

Margery curtsied and wondered wildly if perhaps this brother had been in residence during her disastrous visit. Perhaps *he* spent his time walled up in some closet or attic. But it turned out that Lord Brenton had recently returned from Paris. He exuded an air of disapproval of Margery in particular and bad feelings towards the world in general. After several glasses of the Gardens' famous arrack punch, Lord Brenton suddenly broke into speech.

"What do you think of my breeches?" he demanded.

Amelia surveyed them. "Very fine," she said in a repressive tone of voice. "Margery, do but look at that —"

"Brummell didn't like 'em," said Lord Brenton moodily. " 'How do you like my breeches?' I said. 'My dear fellow, take them off directly,' says Brummell. Ladies present and all. One of the ladies says, 'I beg I may hear of no such thing, else where would he go in his smallclothes?' Told Brummell I'd just got 'em and thought they were rather fine. Know what he said? 'Bad knees, my good fellow! Bad knees!' "

"My lord, your smallclothes are not a subject for the ears of ladies," said Amelia in freezing accents.

But, undeterred, Lord Brenton lumbered to his feet and struck several attitudes. "There! What d'you think? Knees all right, ain't they?"

"Sit *down*, Archie," snapped Toby. "You're embarrassing the ladies."

"Ho! Embarrassing them, am I?" He glared at Margery. "But ain't that the one that Pa said was — Ouch! What did you stamp on my foot for, Toby?"

He sat down abruptly and plunged once more back into a brooding silence.

The bell rang for the fireworks display, and Freddie jumped eagerly to his feet. "Come along, Margery. They've got an extra special display this evening. 'Course, my doctor still says I have to be careful. Says I have Nerves. Says I have Spleen. Says I —"

"We'll come too," said Toby hurriedly, as they joined the press of people moving along the walk.

Margery forgot her troubles in the delight of the fireworks, which burst and flamed and sparkled against the black velvet of the sky. Everyone else in the crowd was sharing her enjoyment, particularly one lady near their group who screamed like a rabbit in the jaws of the weasel at every burst of stars. There were murmurs of amusement and necks twisted and heads turned.

Margery turned her head also and found herself staring straight at the aristocratic profile of her husband. There was another piercing scream, which she realized in a dazed kind of way was coming from the marquess's companion, who was hanging onto his arm.

Mrs. Harrison was in all the glory of a green-and-white striped dress embellished with coquelicot ribbons. She jumped and *oohed* and *aahed* and with every jump her magnificent breasts heaved themselves above her neckline.

Freddie and Toby had seen the marquess at the same moment and were at a loss what to do. But it was Lord Brenton who hailed the marquess in stentorian tones when the display ended, insisting that he join them.

The marquess's eyes held a hectic glitter. "Wouldn't think of it," he murmured. "I am very much engaged."

"Can see that," said Lord Brenton with a roar of drunken laughter. "Some chaps have all the luck, heh!"

"Better go," hissed Freddie, writhing in embarrassment. He tugged at Margery's arm and led the unresisting girl away. There was a long silence.

"Who is she?" asked Margery finally.

"Dashed if I know," said Freddie. "Probably some cousin or relative you don't know," he added, improvising wildly.

"Do you take me for a green goose?" snapped Margery. "That is a lady of the town."

"Well," mumbled Freddie, desperately wishing himself elsewhere, "don't amount to much, you know. All the fellows . . . mean to say . . . wouldn't have brought you here had I known. Oh, damn and blast Charles!"

With dull eyes, Margery noticed the marquess returning to his box. She suddenly clutched Freddie's arm. "Freddie, please go over there and engage Charles in private conversation."

"My dear Margery," said Freddie, with all the enthusiasm of a dissipated sheep. "Not the thing, you know. Just ignore it and we'll go home."

"Please."

"Oh, very well," grumbled Freddie. "But the mood Charles is in, he's going to make me feel no end of an ass!"

Margery sat rigidly watching Freddie's progress. Amelia tried to take her hand and was shrugged off for her pains. Freddie was bowing to Mrs. Harrison. He was saying something. The marquess made some reply and Freddie blushed and made half a move to leave. He caught Margery's watching eye and turned back again. After a few minutes, the marquess gave an impatient shrug and got to his feet. Mrs. Harrison was left alone.

Before Amelia's startled eyes, Margery tripped quickly down from the box and made her way swiftly over to Mrs. Harrison. Toby and his brother watched with their green eyes bulging as never before.

Mrs. Harrison eyed Margery warily. "It's no use you a-making a squawk," she said. "From the looks of you I suppose you're his wife."

"Yes, I am the Marchioness of Edgecombe," said Margery, realizing with a little shock that it was the first time she had used her title.

"It ain't my fault," whined Mrs. Harrison. "I —"

Margery put a hand on her arm. "My dear, I am too used to my husband's — er — pleasures to try now to put a stop to them. I am simply concerned for your welfare."

"Are you threatening me?" demanded the widow, her beautiful eyes narrowing.

"No, indeed," protested Margery. "But you are still young and beautiful and I would not like to see you in the hands of the physicians. My husband, you see, has a certain — er — disorder . . ." Her voice trailed delicately away and she dropped her eyes.

Mrs. Harrison stared at her in alarm.

"Such a fine-looking lord! You mean he has the . . ."

"Exactly," said Margery in a low voice. "He has been in the habit of obtaining his pleasures by promenading the streets of Seven Dials."

"Oh, my Gawd!" One beautiful hand fluttered to Mrs. Harrison's throat.

She knew only too well that certain degenerate members of the aristocracy were in the habit of finding their sexual pleasures in the back alleys of that filthy and notorious slum.

"Oh, my Gawd!" she said again. "You poor thing!"

"As far as I am concerned," said Margery sadly, "the damage has already been done. But I feel for my unfortunate sisters who may not be aware of their peril."

"I'll never forget this," said Mrs. Harrison, wiping her brow. "Anything I can ever do for you, my lady . . ."

"It is enough that you are warned," said Margery, getting hurriedly to her feet. "Please do not tell my husband I have talked with you. He will beat me."

" 'Ere! Letmeoutofthis!" gabbled the suddenly terrified widow. With a tremendous flurry of skirts, she jumped over the back of the box and disappeared. With a grim little smile on her face, Margery returned to her own box. Toby and his brother had their heads together whispering and broke off as

189

soon as they saw her. Amelia seemed to be in a state of shock. Margery wondered how Freddie was coping with her husband.

"Will you stop gabbling and get to the point," the marquess was saying. "We have been walking up and down and up and down and all you can do is bleat."

"No need to talk to me like that," said Freddie, finally breaking into coherent speech. "I ain't a fool, you know."

"No, no," said the marquess in a soothing voice. "You are the veriest wit and a pretty fellow to boot. So out with it!"

Freddie summoned up his courage. "Don't think it right," he said. "Shouldn't be promenading round with that female, and you just wed."

"And you shouldn't be promenading around with my wife," said the marquess, viciously decapitating a rose with his swordstick.

"Not the same thing. No, no, no," said Freddie. "Not the same thing at all. Different. Not at all alike. Opposite. *Vice versa.*"

"Get on with it."

"Well, I'm a gentleman, so that's why it's different. I'm respectable," said Freddie, much struck with this new idea of himself. "Yes. Respectable. *Friend* of Margery's. Now don't tell me *you're* out with that bit of muslin for her conversation," he added with an uncomfortably shrewd look in his weak eyes.

"This is very, very interesting," said the marquess in a deceptively mild voice. "I have known you for years, Freddie, but you surprise me, indeed you do. Pray tell me, what gives you the idea you can preach morality to me?"

Freddie thought about that one very long and carefully. " 'Cause I'm decent and I'm fond of you, and I'm fond of Margery," he said simply.

The marquess shook his head in exasperation. It was like arguing with a nice-natured child.

"Don't worry, old boy," he said impatiently. "Simply attend to your own affairs and leave mine alone."

They had turned about during their conversation and were now back at the boxes, which were crammed to capacity with the exception of one.

"You may rest easy," drawled the marquess. "My ladybird has flown." He made a distant bow in the direction of Margery's box and took his leave, wondering all the while why Mrs. Harrison had left and why he should feel so relieved.

The following morning, a light waft of delicate fragrance assailed the marquess's nostrils. He put down the morning paper and regarded his wife with some surprise. Had last night's humiliations meant nothing to her? She should have at least had the decency to breakfast in her room.

"Good morning, Charles," said the marchioness brightly, shaking out her napkin.

"Good morning, madam wife," replied the marquess genially. "Which one of my friends are you going to commandeer as escort today?"

"I haven't had time to think," replied Margery placidly. "Probably Toby. He mentioned something about driving in the park. Don't grind your teeth, dear. It does wear down the enamel so. Then there is the Choldomeley ball tonight, but then, with your many diversions, I do not suppose you will be present."

"We shall *both* be present . . . together. If you have no care for appearances, then I most certainly have."

"You have a *very* odd way of showing it, sir," said Margery with the same infuriating calm. "I must have been dreaming during my seasons or else the world has changed. I was under the impression that any gentleman who flaunted his inamorata in front of his wife was in danger of being castigated as a *shabby dog.*"

"I did not know you would be at Vauxhall."

"Oh, indeed!" said Margery sweetly. "That *does* make a difference."

"Don't fence with me," said the marquess

192

in a thin voice. He threw down the paper and strode to the door, fully aware that his wife was about to attack a hearty breakfast with all the appearance of not having a care in the world.

He turned in the doorway. "I shall expect your company at eight of the clock, madam."

"Very good, my lord," said his wife demurely.

There was a stifled exclamation from behind her and the door closed with a crash.

Margery shut her eyes and gritted her teeth to fight down the sudden wave of pain which threatened to engulf her.

Resplendent in evening dress, the marquess sat in the drawing room that evening with the decanter for company and waited for his wife.

He raised his eyebrows as Freddie was ushered into the room. "What the hell are you doing here?" snapped the marquess. "Am I not to be allowed to escort my own wife?"

"Steady on," said Freddie nervously. "I've called to escort Lady Amelia."

"Aha!" said the marquess sourly. "If you can't drool over my wife you will settle for her nearest and dearest."

"You're like a dog with a bone," said Freddie amiably. "But the fact is, I like Lady Amelia. Know where I am with her. Know what to expect. Widow, ain't she? Well, then . . ."

The marquess raised his quizzing glass. "Lady Amelia is at least twenty years your senior."

"Getting very nice in your tastes, ain't you?" said Freddie, with a sneer sitting oddly on his normally amiable features.

Both friends glared at each other like two tomcats squaring up to fight.

The marquess gave a sudden shrug and pushed the decanter across the table. "Help yourself, Freddie," he said in a more friendly tone of voice. "I don't know what has come over me. Women are the very devil."

To his surprise, Freddie refused to drink, and he realized that it had been some time since he had seen his friend in his usual half-intoxicated condition.

At that moment his wife walked into the room followed by Lady Amelia. Margery was wearing a violet satin slip of a gown with an overdress of gold gauze. Small white rosebuds had been twined into her hair, and she wore one magnificent white rose on her bosom. There was an almost ethereal air about her, and the marquess caught his breath. She had never looked more beautiful. He remembered the feel of her arms round his neck and the silk of her skin. A flood of emotions assailed him all at once — anger, jealousy, passion, and possessiveness — and out of them all, love rose like a pale ghost and hovered in the stuffy overfurnished drawing room, where the

Edgecombe ancestors seemed to stare down in perpetual surprise at the weakness of their descendant.

Then she touched the rose at her bosom and smiled. "Isn't it pretty? And so *kind* of Perry. He sent me such a pretty poem, as well. How did it go, Amelia?

'Aske me no more where Jove bestowes,
When June is past, the fading rose;
For in your beautie's orient deepe
These flowers, as in their causes, sleepe.' "

"How lovely," sighed Lady Amelia. "Quite in the Elizabethan manner."

"It should be," drawled the marquess. "It was written by an Elizabethan — one Thomas Carew. I would not have credited Swanley with plagiarism."

"He didn't *say* it was his own," said his wife crossly. " 'Tis very affecting, nonetheless. Shall we go?"

His newfound love for Margery had made the marquess more than ever determined to hurt her in some way. How dare she sit so calm and smiling while he sighed and suffered? Perhaps the Choldomeley ball would supply an opportunity.

And opportunity presented itself almost as soon as they had entered the ballroom, in the voluptuous shape of Lady Camberwell.

Lady Cecilia Camberwell had enjoyed many

affairs and liaisons. She had an unassailable social position and a knack for discretion. She had outlasted a score of lovers and two husbands. Although nearly in her fortieth year, she was a magnificent figure of a woman with a creamy skin and masses of midnight-black hair. Her lazy smile was a seduction in itself. The marquess knew she was searching for a new *amour*. He abandoned his wife and marched purposefully off in Lady Camberwell's direction.

Margery danced determinedly with Toby (who breathed heavily in her face and trod on her feet) with his brother, Lord Brenton (overly familiar) and only once with Freddie, who seemed to prefer to join Lady Amelia in the row of chaperones. Viscount Swanley had not put in an appearance.

Viscount Swanley arrived only when the supper bell was rung. An Indian summer had been warming London's autumn, and tables had been set up in a marquee in the garden. The marquee was very grand, being made of purple silk with its sides raised up on gold poles rather in the manner of an exotic Oriental tent. Margery was therefore afforded an excellent view of her husband vanishing into a rose-strewn arbor with Lady Camberwell.

Margery gathered the attention of her audience, which consisted of Freddie and Lady Amelia, Toby and his brother, and Viscount Swanley. She pointed her fork in the direction of the arbor into which her husband had just disappeared.

"That arbor is vastly pretty. But it is too late for roses to be growing, outside of a succession house. They must be made of silk."

"Clever, that," said Freddie indifferently.

"I would like them," said Margery, examining a lobster pattie.

"Eh!" said all of the gentlemen in chorus.

"I would like them . . . all those roses," said Margery dreamily. "I have often wondered what it would be like to have masses and masses of roses."

"I say," expostulated Toby. "Can't go around picking roses in the middle of the ball."

Margery pouted prettily. "If it were a bet you would do it without thinking."

That magic word "bet" roused the gentlemen as if they were warhorses scenting the smell of battle.

"Wager you an hundred guineas," said Toby, much flushed, "that I can pick the most."

"Done," cried Perry and Lord Brenton. Freddie for once was silent.

To the amazement of the other guests, the three contestants plunged into the arbor with loud whoops and yells and started grabbing enormous handfuls of artificial roses. There was a feminine squeal and a masculine oath and the marquess and Lady Camberwell emerged from the arbor. Like Margery, she had been wearing white roses in her hair, and one of the enthusiastic contestants had grabbed at them in the darkness of the arbor, mistaking them for part of the decoration. Lady Camberwell caught the hard stare of Margery's eye and flushed angrily. She had no desire to have her latest flirt broadcast to the world in general and to this formidable little wife in particular.

The marquess had disappeared, but Lady Camberwell moved towards Margery's table. The contestants were still whooping and yelling and seizing handfuls of roses.

Lady Camberwell had talked her way out of many scandals, and there was no doubt in her mind that she could sooth this wife's ruffled feelings. She accordingly sat down beside Margery with great aplomb and gave a pretty laugh. "The Marchioness of Edgecombe, is it not? You must excuse me for borrowing your husband. I am a great bird fancier and I was sure there was a white owl nesting in that arbor. But alas! It must have been the roses all the time."

"My husband is a bird fancier too," said Margery sweetly. "I am not surprised at his enthusiasm. He has a great interest in birds of all shapes and plumage. I unfortunately do not share his interest although I take a slight interest in each bird he happens to fancy — their plumage, their habits, their different little cries. We have a *very* modern marriage and he talks freely about his — er — feathered friends. Then when conversation flags, *I* tell all *my* friends about his birds, and they are kind enough to show a most flattering interest."

Lady Camberwell gave a lazy laugh. "Come now. All the world knows that Charles never discusses his . . . hobbies."

"Ah, but that was before he was married," said Margery, looking straight into Lady Camberwell's beautiful eyes. The gentlemen were triumphantly piling up roses at their feet, but their actions went unheeded.

Lady Camberwell gave a little nod and then rose to her feet. "A most interesting discussion, my lady," she said. "It is as well we were only talking about birds. Gossip, in this society of ours, can be a dangerous thing."

"Indeed it can," replied Margery earnestly. "Only think how they applaud a *man* who has many lovers, and smile indulgently and call him a rake. But a *lady* . . . ah, now, there's the rub. Gossip like that could tear her reputation to shreds an' you take my meaning."

"Perfectly," said Lady Camberwell with a tight little smile. As she moved away, she heard Freddie bleating, "I didn't know Charles was interested in birds," and Lady Amelia's warning *Hush.*

Lady Camberwell met the marquess at the

entrance to the ballroom. His mocking smile glinted down at her. "Do you come with me, my lady?" he whispered. "We did not finish our discussion."

He looked so handsome. Lady Camberwell gave a mental little sigh of regret. "I have the headache, Charles," she said firmly. "You must excuse me." She pushed past him almost rudely.

He looked after her with his eyes narrowed and then shrugged. He would lie in *some* woman's arms tonight, no matter who, to try to assuage this aching desire for revenge.

He looked across the lawn to his wife. She was sitting surrounded by masses and masses of white roses. A light breeze was lifting her hair and her face was alive with amusement as she listened to Viscount Swanley. The marquess swore under his breath. There was always Mrs. Harrison.

Toby and his brother jolted home together in the confines of a closed carriage. "Know what?" asked Lord Brenton, suddenly breaking the silence. "She's hot stuff!"

"Hold on," said Toby angrily. "If you mean Lady Margery, then you're wrong."

"Pooh!" said Lord Brenton. "You know and I know that Charles was fooling around in the shrubbery with Lady Camberwell. Margery knew it and she didn't turn a hair. Welcomed the woman to the table and prattled on about birdwatching. She'll soon be looking for her own lover."

"Not Margery!"

"Yes, Margery! Pa was right, you know. He said he could always tell the flighty ones. Think about it, Toby. I can tell by the way she looks at you."

Toby thought. It was a painful process, since he was not in the habit of thinking very much about anything.

"I couldn't . . . she wouldn't," he said finally.

Lord Brenton nudged him in the ribs and winked fatly in the darkness of the carriage. "Take it from your elder brother," he said. "She *could* and she *would*."

The Marquess of Edgecombe presented his card to a trim parlor maid at a slim house in Half Moon Street and requested her to inform Mrs. Harrison that she had a late visitor.

"Very good, my lord," said the girl, scurrying up the stairs and throwing the handsome lord an appreciative look over her shoulder.

There was a murmur of voices from above and a sudden shriek of *"No!"*

A few minutes later, the parlor maid came hurrying down the stairs with her eyes lowered. "Please, my lord. Mrs. Harrison, she isn't home."

"I see," said the marquess, slowly reflecting that he did not. He took his hat and cane from where he had so confidently thrown them on the sofa and made his way out into the night. First Lady Camberwell, and now this!

He must be losing his touch.

Chapter Twelve

With an abrupt change in the weather, fog and frost descended on the streets of London: thick, yellow, choking fog which crept into the clubs and drawing rooms, soiling the Brussels lace of the curtains and bringing with it a marrow-freezing chill.

Lady Margery felt immeasurably listless and depressed. She and her husband moved about their town mansion like polite strangers. The chilling weather had allayed the ripe smell of the sewers, but little else could be found in its favor. The marquess's frozen manner seemed an extension of the weather itself. Margery had flirted gaily with Toby and Lord Brenton and Viscount Swanley and even Freddie — although the latter seemed to spend most of his time in Amelia's company — but to all this the marquess seemed to turn a blind eye.

Toby was particularly gratified by Margery's attentions and felt he was changing into quite a ladies' man. He affected large nosegays in his buttonhole and had even taken to wearing scent and — wonder of wonders — confessed to having baths at least twice a month. His sporting cronies shook their heads over this, prophesying everything from pneumonia to the plague, and Toby would have dropped this new fashion had not Freddie and Viscount Swanley confessed that they themselves took baths regularly, and as for the marquess, it was rumored that he took a bath almost every day!

That was enough for Toby. He had no intention of going to such extremes as Edgecombe, but on the other hand he had actually begun to *enjoy* his twice-monthly immersion in hot water. And, as he confided to the marquess, it certainly kept the dashed livestock at bay and he didn't want to end up like old Ellington, whose wig crawled like a zoo!

Margery began to feel that her life had always been the same, as grim winter settled over London. Sometimes she felt that she, Margery, was the chaperone and Amelia the debutante as Lady Amelia attended more and more balls and parties, always escorted by the ever-attentive Freddie.

"How *kind* Freddie is," thought Margery. "Not many young men would take such trouble to be kind to a middle-aged lady."

The marquess also felt that his life had become stale, flat, and unprofitable. The pain Margery's appearance caused him had remained undiminished, but he had no longer tried to set up an affair with any other woman.

He was brooding over this one evening while the yellow snakes of fog wound themselves round his library and his wife was off somewhere dancing in the arms of some other man. He prowled moodily along the bookshelves, searching for something to read to pass the long hours before bedtime.

A wisp of lace at the corner of the sofa caught his eye and he stopped his pacing to pick it up. It was one of Margery's handkerchiefs. Without thinking, he raised it to his nose, smelling the light fragrance she usually wore. He was suddenly attacked by such a rush of passion that he crumpled the fine linen and lace in his fingers into a ball and threw it back on the sofa.

Damn her!

He thought of Mrs. Harrison again and wondered why she had refused to see him. He mounted the steps to his dressing room three at a time and jerked open a drawer in his dresser. He picked out a small jewel box and opened it. A small flower made of sapphires and diamonds winked up at him in the candlelight. He had bought it as a gift for Margery and had never given it to her. He rang the bell and sat down at a desk and began to write hurriedly.

When the servant replied to his summons, he handed him the jewel box and a note and told him to deliver it to Mrs. Harrison in Half Moon Street immediately.

"And if that doesn't fetch her, nothing will," thought the marquess grimly. He walked downstairs to the library to wait.

His answer arrived in a remarkably short time. Mrs. Harrison thanked his lordship for his munificent gift and was desirous of having a few words with him.

His only thought as he shrugged himself into his benjamin and collected his curly-brimmed beaver and cane was one of triumph. No longer would he sit around his home waiting for the sound of his wife's step on the stairs like a lovesick youth.

Mrs. Harrison was as seductive as he had remembered, but to his surprise he was ushered into the drawing room instead of being taken straight to the bedroom.

After a brief exchange of pleasantries, the widow fell silent and sat twisting her handkerchief in her plump, beringed hands. She was wearing his gift at her bosom and the gems winked and sparkled in the light.

The marquess was about to make a general remark about the weather, to end the awkward silence, when Mrs. Harrison burst out with, "I can't believe it, my lord. I can't!"

The marquess's thin brows snapped together. "What can't you believe?"

"That you've got what . . . what she said you 'ad . . . had."

"Who is *she?*" snapped the marquess.

"Your wife," said Mrs. Harrison simply.

"You are mistaken. You have not met my wife. Come, my dear, we have more pleasant things to discuss."

Mrs. Harrison shrank back against the sofa cushions. "But I *did* . . . meet your wife," she protested. "It was at Vauxhall when you went off with that other fellow, the stupid-looking one."

The marquess easily identified Freddie from this unflattering description and he began to remember. He remembered Freddie's uncharacteristic insistence on a "private coze" and Mrs. Harrison's sudden disappearance.

"Tell me what she said," he asked.

His face was very white and stern, and Mrs. Harrison was beginning to regret her greed in accepting the brooch. She began to babble. "She said as how you was in the habit of a-taking your pleasures in Seven Dials and she said . . . she said you 'ad the . . ."

"Did she say I had the pox?" asked the marquess incredulously.

Mrs. Harrison nodded dumbly.

"The intriguing little minx," said the marquess slowly. "The jade!"

Mrs. Harrison looked at him with a dawning glimmer of hope. "You mean her ladyship was lying?"

"Of course she was lying," said the marquess savagely. "Do I look as if I need to find my pleasures in the most squalid slum in London?"

Mrs. Harrison eyed him appreciatively, from his impeccably tailored evening coat to his breeches and silk stockings and the fine fall of old lace at his neck and wrists.

"No, that you don't," she said on a sigh. "And to think, your lady had me really scared. She must love you very much."

"What a strange idea of love . . . going round telling the world and his wife that I have the pox," snarled the marquess.

Mrs. Harrison opened her mouth to point out that Lady Margery had only been trying to break up her husband's latest flirt, but closed her mouth again. A happily married man was not in her own interests.

The marquess mentally picked his little wife up by the throat and banged her head against the wall. Outwardly, he smiled slowly into the widow's eyes and said softly, "We are wasting valuable time."

Toby, his brother Archie, and Perry were, at that moment, sitting over their forgotten drinks in Watier's, staring at Freddie in amazement.

Toby was the first to find his voice. "Marry!" he said. "You! Marry Lady Amelia. You must be mad. She's old enough to be your mother!"

"He's right," said Viscount Swanley. "Not the thing at all, Freddie. They'll say you've got the same weird tastes as Prinny. He likes his game well hung."

Freddie wished he had not spoken. How could he explain the attractions of a placid smile, a beautiful pair of shoulders, a warm feeling of having come home at last?

"Don't like the company she keeps, either," said Lord Archie suddenly. "Lady Margery ain't all she should be."

"Steady on!" cried Perry.

"Well, she ain't," said Archie stubbornly. "Led you all a fine dance, didn't she? I'm told, moreover, that Amelia Carroll ain't got a feather to fly with. Stands to reason she'd snap up a rich young man."

"There will be no more discussion on the subject," said Freddie firmly. "But as far as Margery is concerned, I don't think her marriage is very happy, and she is simply using us to escort her to balls and functions because her husband will not."

Freddie got to his feet and gave his friends a quaint little dignified bow. "Furthermore I'm going to avoid your company until you learn to speak of my lady friends with a bit more respect."

He marched away, leaving the three to look after him. "It's the wine," said Toby after a long silence. "Finally addled his wits."

"He ain't been drinking at all," drawled

Perry. "I wrote a poem about it. It goes like this:

" 'Oh, Serpent in the goblet cup —' "

"How can it be a 'goblet cup'?" sneered Archie. "It's either one or t'other."

"It's known as poetic license," said Perry stiffly. The pair of them began to squabble in a halfhearted way, leaving Toby to his jumbled thoughts. Earlier in the evening, Archie had again been hinting that Margery could be his for the asking. "Of course, she'll play all coy," Archie had said. "Girls like that like a show of force. Saves face, as the Chinamen say. Bet if you swept her away to some cozy little nest, she'd cry and struggle just for show and then she'd just melt in your arms."

No lady had ever melted in Toby's arms, and the thought awakened a lot of old dormant feudal fevers. Vague ideas for an abduction began to form in his mind, aided by the old French brandy in front of him and by the unreality engendered by the thick bands of yellow fog which were floating across the clubroom.

Thoughts raced and chased each other through his head with all the rapidity of Lord Alvanley running the mile in under six minutes along the Edgware Road. The dandy set were deep in games of macao, losing and gaining fortunes with well-bred ease. Brummell had brought elegance and cleanliness to these young men, many of whom had served in the army with great gallantry. They were witty, amusing, and urbane, and Toby envied them from the bottom of his country heart. He affected the dandy style of dress himself but fell short of Brummell's maxim that a true dandy should be inconspicuous in his dress. Toby's squat, burly figure was not made for fashionable lean lines, and it had taken the efforts of three footmen to get him into his coat. He was wearing his cravat in the *mathematical,* a style with three creases in it, *couleur de la cuisse d'une nymphe émue.* He had felt all the crack when he had surveyed himself in the long glass before leaving his lodgings, but now the image that peered back at him from one of the large mirrors on the other side of the room showed him a depressing picture of a bucolic squire lately come to town. He sighed heavily and his Cumberland corset let out a protesting squeak. How could he be expected to seduce anyone? His coat was so tight that he could hardly raise his arms.

The Marquess of Edgecombe came awake with a start, climbing up through fathomless pits of sleep. The watch was crying the hour on the street outside. Two o'clock in the morning. He fumbled for his tinderbox and in the dim light of the dying fire saw a candle beside the bed and lit it.

He felt absolutely dreadful. Mrs. Harrison

had performed her part well, and with each heave and sigh and groan he had tried to blot out the memory of other lips against his own, fresh and generous. He lay among the relics of his dead passion and felt miserable. His partner turned sleepily in the large bed and the acrid aroma of stale sweat and heavy musk assailed his nostrils. He had meant somehow to revenge himself on Margery, but he was left the sufferer.

The candle flame grew brighter, illuminating the frowsty, cluttered room. A great wind heaved and racked the buildings and streets of London, stealing icy fingers of cold into the bedroom and sending weird shadows dancing on the walls.

The heavy silk of the bed hangings moved gently and he found himself staring straight at a large cockroach. It clung to the silken hangings, glittering, fat, and obscene, and the marquess shivered suddenly with a mixture of repulsion, distaste, and cold.

He had frequented many bedrooms such as this, but never before had he endured such self-disgust. He climbed slowly from the bed so as not to disturb the figure sleeping beside him.

How triumphantly he had lain here a few hours before, waiting for her to undress. She had posed seductively, striking various attitudes in the manner of her kind as her maid had removed her outer garments. He had felt virile, amused, in command of the situation. Then the maid had been dismissed, after loosening her mistress's stays.

The heavy stays had fallen to the floor and the marquess had closed his eyes in sudden pain. It seemed as if great mounds of white flesh had been released from their prison. The vision of his wife's slim, high-breasted body had flashed before his eyes to taunt him. That was what had made him go through with it, he decided.

The wind outside tore furiously at the shutters, bringing with it a picture of clean, wild country and pure air. He made up his mind. He would call on his father and stay with him. He would then travel abroad and stay away from England until the hurt caused by the humiliation of his marriage had healed.

He dressed quietly and quickly and let himself softly out of the bedroom.

The wind roared along Half Moon Street and there was an almighty crash as a chimney stack was blown clear from its mooring and came crashing down onto the cobbles. A small moon racing high above, between ragged clouds, emphasized his sudden feeling of loneliness. He would go to Watier's and drink and talk and perhaps play macao until the pain lessened, and then he would ride to his father's estate.

Some remnants of fog still clung in the

corners of the cardroom. He sat down heavily beside Toby Sanderson and called for brandy. Toby was still in conversation with Perry and Archie, and all betrayed by their cautious speech and movements that they had been drinking heavily.

"Been amusing yourself, Charles?" queried Archie with a leer.

The marquess gave him a cold look, drank off a bumper of brandy in one gulp, and turned to Toby.

"I thought you might be with my wife this evening, Toby," he remarked lightly. He drained another bumper of brandy.

Toby looked at the marquess nervously. "Not me," he said hurriedly.

"That makes a change," said the marquess in the same deceptively light voice. His three friends watched as another liberal glass of brandy followed the first two down the marquess's throat.

The marquess became aware of a smell of bad drainage from somewhere behind him. "Hallo, Ellington," he remarked without bothering to turn his head.

"Glad to see you're fit and well," said Lord Ellington while they all hurriedly buried their faces in their scented handkerchiefs. Dear God, thought Perry, Ellington gets riper by the minute. "I was walking along Half Moon Street," continued Lord Ellington, as usual blissfully unaware of the effect of his aroma, "and I saw you nearly getting hit by a dashed great chimney pot. Ah, well, the devil looks after his own, and talkin' about devils, wasn't that the fair Harrison's house you was coming out of?"

"So?" said the marquess, helping himself generously from the decanter.

Lord Ellington slapped him on the back with one grimy hand. " 'So,' he says. What a dog you are, Charles! Newly wed and all and still sampling the delights of the night."

"You see, my wife understands me completely," said the marquess simply. He felt he had just said something wrong, for Perry was looking at him strangely, but the brandy was affecting his brain very quickly and he had a sudden desire to make bad worse.

"A toast to my beautiful wife," said the marquess, getting to his feet. "A toast to the modern woman. I allow my wife the same liberty as I allow myself. Come, gentlemen! You are not drinking."

"See! *See!*" whispered Archie, nudging Toby so violently that he spilled some of his drink on the table.

A black servant deftly mopped it up and then stood close by to be on hand. In his experience, a table such as this would soon put more brandy on the floor than in their mouths. Ah, well, only a few more years and he would be able to open his public house in the East End.

Ellington laughed noisily and strolled away, leaving the members of the table to put down their handkerchiefs and sigh with relief.

"Weird weather," commented Perry conversationally. "First demned fog, then demned storm. It reminds me of —"

"The modern woman," said the marquess, paying no attention. "They want their freedom? Then let 'em have it. God knows, there are enough female rakes in this society of ours."

Archie leaned forward with his protruding eyes gleaming. "You should not talk so of your wife in public," he said, carefully adding another brand to the marquess's fire. "Respectable lady, your wife."

"Pah!" said the marquess with a hectic glint in his eye. "That one is any man's for the taking."

As soon as the words were out of his mouth, he would have given anything to take them back. He looked wildly round at his friends and wondered if he were going mad. Mumbling some incoherent good-evenings, he all but ran from the club.

"Pay no attention," said Perry. "Charles is drunk."

"*In vino veritas*, heh, Toby?" said Archie slyly.

"Oh, tol rol," said Toby, waving his fat fingers in the air in a sort of dismissive way. But already his brain was busy. Hadn't

Charles practically given him *leave* to seduce Margery? It looked as if his, Toby's, earlier ideas of women were right. They were minxes all. Sighing and simpering and protesting gentility while all the while they were no better than that Mrs. Harrison. He thought of clasping a yielding Margery in his arms — in a looser coat, of course — and felt no end of a buck.

He came to a sudden decision. "Heh, Archie, 'member what you was suggesting? Well, I have a plan. Sorry, Perry, not for your ears."

He moved closer to Archie and bent his great head and began to whisper. Perry drank idly until snatches of their conversation began to reach his ears: ". . . gamekeeper's cottage . . . deserted . . . grounds of Tuttering . . . Lady Margery . . ."

Perry stiffened. They wouldn't, they couldn't! He suddenly decided to call on Charles in the morning and warn him that his ill-advised remarks may have put wrong ideas in the fat heads of a certain pair of country gentlemen.

The marquess reined in his horse and looked down at the shabby figure crouched over a flower bed near the entrance to the ducal estate of Delham. The figure wore a shabby tweed coat and its head was covered with a stained and battered tricorne. Nonetheless, he had no difficulty in recognizing his father, the tenth Duke of Pelham.

"Hullo, father," said the marquess, dismounting from his horse.

The duke's aged, weatherbeaten face peered up at him curiously for a few seconds and then his blue eyes, very like his son's, cleared in recognition.

"Charles, my boy," said the duke, with a marked lack of paternal enthusiasm. "Have you finally brought Margery to see me?"

"No, father. My wife is occupied in town."

"Well, well, well. Seems odd to me. Not allowed to see my own daughter-in-law. But come inside and we'll talk."

The duke cast a longing look back at the flower bed, heaved a heavy sigh, and trotted up to Delham Court beside the tall figure of his son.

The great house was much as Charles had remembered it from childhood, dim and silent and redolent of dry rot and damp dogs.

"Come in, my boy. Come in," said the duke, leading the way into a ground-floor saloon. "Now we can be cozy."

The marquess's lips twisted in a wry smile. The vast, chilly saloon stretched into infinity and a minuscule fire of sea coal flared on the vast black hearth. The duke pottered from side to side of the great saloon, picked up a gardening book, removed his hat, straightened his wig with one earthy finger, and to all in-

218

tents and purposes forgot about his son's existence.

The marquess sighed. It was always a mistake to come back. Always a mistake to come searching for the home that had never really existed outside his imagination. As a boy, he had rarely seen either his father or mother, having been brought up by the nurse, then the tutor, then Eton and Oxford, and then another tutor to take him away on the Grand Tour. His mother had died when he was at Oxford, and he was ashamed because he had been more upset over the death of his old nurse. His head throbbed and ached from the effects of the brandy and he longed for bed.

He gave a gentle cough, but his father remained immersed in his book. Charles looked at him sadly for a minute or two and then got to his feet and quietly left the room.

The duke was vaguely aware later that someone had arrived and that he should perhaps be arranging something for their comfort. But after all, that was what one kept servants for. He returned to his book.

The marquess slept long and heavily, only awakening as a fiery sunset burned out the end of the winter's day. The rooks were wheeling and diving over the bare brown fields. Trees threw their skeletal arms up to the red and blazing sky like lost souls stretching up out of hell.

Faintly, somewhere in the great house, the marquess heard the sound of the dressing gong. His father was a stickler for protocol, and he would be expected to present himself attired in evening coat and knee breeches for dinner.

As he rummaged through his jewel box, he thought of the brooch he had so carelessly bestowed on Mrs. Harrison. If only there were *someone*, just anyone, to confide in. But one did not share the secrets of the marriage bed with one's friends.

Dinner was a long and solemn affair. Father and son sat at either end of a long polished table. The duke had his book propped against the saltcellar.

Remove followed remove until at last the port and nuts were brought in and the army of servants withdrew.

"Father!" said the marquess in an imperative tone.

The duke looked along the length of the table until he realized that his son and heir was seated at the other. He carefully and reluctantly marked his place in the book. "Hallo, Charles," he said genially. "When did you arrive?"

"I arrived this morning," said the marquess testily, "and before you forget my existence again, perhaps you would favor me with your attention."

"Of course, of course, my boy," said the

duke, his eyes staring longingly at his book.

The marquess picked up the decanter and strolled languidly down the length of the table and drew up a chair next to his father. He gently lifted the book from the saltcellar and turned it face down on the table, ignoring his father's annoyance and distress.

"You're going to ask me for money," said the duke almost pettishly.

"I have plenty of money of my own," pointed out the marquess.

"Then what else can you want?" asked the duke patiently.

"Strange as it may seem," said the marquess slowly, "I would like to hear what my mother was like."

The duke stared at him in surprise and then turned to stare at a portrait of his wife, which hung above the fireplace, as if expecting the painted mouth to open.

"Well, there she is," he said, waving a feeble hand to introduce the portrait. "Ain't as if she died when you was a child."

"But I never knew her, you see," said the marquess gently. "I saw her very briefly during my childhood — and you too, sir, for that matter."

"That's natural," protested the duke, retreating behind his favorite argument. "That's what servants are for. You had the best nurse, the best tutors."

The duke stared myopically into his glass.

"Alicia," he said at last. "Pretty name. I still miss her, my boy. Still miss her. People thought she was a cold, autocratic woman. But she wasn't, at least not with me."

He stared again at his glass, again forgetting his son's existence and talking almost as if to himself. "Fire and passion, that's what she was."

His son stiffened suddenly.

"Fire and passion," mused the duke, his face alight with memories. A log fell in the fireplace and sent a sudden sheet of flame up the chimney, and the wind began to rise again outside.

"We were lucky, very lucky," the old voice went on. "It was a suitable match, but a love match for all that. I had everything a man could desire, a handsome wife in the drawing room and a passionate seductress in the bedroom."

"But surely women — society women — are not supposed to — er — behave with any abandon in the bedroom," said the marquess in a husky voice.

"Eh, what?" said the duke. "Oh, hallo, Charles."

"Father," said the marquess, slowly and patiently. "It is important for me to know . . . for you to tell me. I had thought that women of our class did not indulge in strong passions."

"Why not?" asked the duke, looking properly at his son for the first time. "Women are the same all over, ain't they? You can't say we neglected your education along those lines. Didn't I fix you up with the best courtesan in London soon as you were old enough? Didn't she teach you anything?"

"She taught me that an experienced woman can supply what she is paid for," he said dryly. "After that I had one abortive affair with a certain society lady, and the fire and passion that she gave to me meant all the world. I gave her my love and my heart. In return she supplied that fire and passion to several lovers apart from me, with happy, carefree indiscrimination. When I taxed her with it, she laughed in my face and called me a green boy. Since that time I have paid for my pleasures.

"A wife . . . well, I expected nothing more than that she should comport herself properly and supply me with an heir. On our wedding night, she seemed to burn in my arms. And I was shocked. No gently nurtured female should show such abandon."

"Fiddle," said his father. "It's all the fault of your damned Methodist-ridden generation, your milk-and-water misses. In my day, we expected our women to match our passions."

A slow feeling of panic began to grip the marquess.

"Had you told me this earlier —" he began wrathfully.

The duke picked up his book. "How was I to know you would be so stupid?" he countered.

He pulled a branch of candles nearer and proceeded to read, unaware that he had rocked his son's well-ordered world to its very foundations.

Unnoticed by his father, the marquess rose and left the table. He must return to London as soon as possible. He had behaved like a fool. Some of the remarks he had made at Watier's seemed to burn into his mind as he groaned aloud.

The duke mistook his anguish for indigestion.

"Try rhubarb cordial," he said kindly. "Best thing. Works every time."

But the duke spoke to empty air.

The marquess had gone.

Lady Margery smiled sweetly at the gentleman on the sofa next to her. "Pray go on, sir," she said. "Ormolu interests me vastly."

Her companion plunged into a long dissertation and Margery smiled and nodded, her thoughts elsewhere. Why had she decided to attend this party? There was no need now that there was no husband to mark her absence. Someone over by the window exclaimed that it had started to snow, and she let out a little sigh of relief. That would be a good excuse to leave early. She looked round for Lady Amelia, but as usual her companion had disappeared, no doubt on the arm of Mr. Freddie Jamieson. She envied them their comfortable friendship.

Had she but known, Freddie was feeling anything but comfortable as he rose from his knees and stared at Amelia in dismay. "But I say," he expostulated. "After all, why *not* get married?"

Amelia looked up at him, her eyes bright with unshed tears. How could she explain that it was impossible for a woman of her years to marry such a young man? How he would regret it when she was an old woman and he still in his prime? "Say no more to-night, Freddie," she whispered. "I would not have anything spoil our friendship."

"But dash it all," said Freddie. "I want more than friendship."

Amelia looked at his fair and foolish face. She had learned to love this bashful and sometimes stupid young man as she had never loved anyone before. Why should they not have a discreet liaison? Would he be shocked? But that way they should have a little time together. She looked up at him appealingly and opened her mouth.

"Freddie!"

But it was not Amelia who had called his name. Viscount Swanley was standing in the doorway. His clothes were mud-stained and his hair was tousled.

He strode into the room. "It's Toby," he gasped. "He's gone mad. I think he's just abducted Lady Margery."

Amelia leapt to her feet, her own worries forgotten.

"You must be mistaken," said Freddie soothingly. "Toby would never do a thing like that."

"But he *has*, I tell you," yelled Perry. "I wasn't coming here at all. I passed his traveling carriage on the road and I thought I heard someone screaming. Well, I had overheard Toby and his brother plotting something, but I didn't pay much notice 'cause I thought they were in their cups. Then I remembered Margery was here and I thought I'd call in and make sure. Fellow she was talking to last, he says Toby comes up and says it's starting to snow and that you, Lady Amelia, are already waiting in his carriage.

"She goes into the carriage and then cries out, 'Amelia isn't here!' The door is slammed and the carriage races off."

Amelia had gone very white.

"We'll chase 'em," said Freddie. "Do you know where they have gone?"

"Toby said something last night about a deserted gamekeeper's cottage at Tuttering."

"My wagon is faster," said Freddie. "Let's go."

"I'm coming with you," cried Amelia.

"Better let 'er," said Perry gloomily. "With

any luck, we may be able to save Margery's reputation."

"Just what was that about my wife's reputation?" said a cold voice from the door.

Impeccable in evening dress, the tall figure of the Marquess of Edgecombe stood in the doorway.

His two friends leapt on him and hustled him outside. "No time to tell you, Charles," gasped Freddie. "Tell you on the road."

Chapter Thirteen

Margery struggled against the stifling gag, staring at Toby with horror. This could not be nineteenth-century England!

He had been so solicitous, so convincing at the party. When she had put her head inside his carriage and found it empty and had turned round to protest, she had received a vicious shove which had sent her sprawling forward among the straw on the floor. Toby had jumped in after her and tried to gather her in his arms as the carriage lurched forward. She had fought and struggled and screamed for nearly a mile until Toby had taken out a large Belcher handkerchief and ruthlessly gagged her and bound her hands.

From the strong smell of brandy on her companion's breath, Margery realized with dismay that he had fortified himself for the ordeal.

She was disheveled and shivering and her cloak and dress were torn.

Toby sat sulkily nursing his scratched face. It had not turned out the way he had expected, and he felt a dull resentment against the world in general. He fortified himself from his flask and began to feel more cheerful. As soon as he reached Tuttering, he would have all night to exercise the considerable masculine charm his brother has assured him he had.

Then he noticed that the coach, which had previously been hurtling along at a great rate, had slowed considerably. He let down the window and leaned his head out and asked his coachman what the deuce he meant by dawdling at this cursed pace. A blizzard was blowing full strength and the coachman's protesting voice came faintly through the storm. If he went any faster they would end in the ditch, he said.

"Spring 'em!" snapped Toby, slamming the window up again. The coach gave a great lurch and bounded forward.

Frantic thoughts chased each other round in Margery's brain. If only he would remove the gag, then perhaps she could plead with him. What would her husband say?

As if in answer to her unspoken query, Toby said, "It ain't no use you sitting there looking at me as if I was some sort of monster. No use pretending to be so hoity-toity either. Charles told me about you. Said you was any man's for the asking."

Margery realized with a dull surprise that hearts did break. How else could she explain the great wrenching pain in her bosom?

Never until now had she lost hope of

somehow gaining her husband's affections. The carriage lurched and swayed and the wind howled and screamed.

"I hope we crash," thought Margery wretchedly. "I wish I were dead."

As if in answer to her prayer, there came a great cry from the roof of the coach, a sound of splintering wood, and she was thrown across the carriage on top of Toby as the whole carriage overturned on its side.

She wriggled away from him and tried to stand up. Her hands had been tied loosely behind her and she found that with the tremendous jolt they had worked free. She unloosened her gag and relieved her feelings with a spate of unmaidenly language culled from the hunting field. There was no reply. The free door of the carriage was now above her, and it suddenly swung open and a footman's white and anxious face peered in.

"Mr. Sanderson?" queried the servant. "We're in the ditch, sir. John coachman said you made him take the road too fast and it's snowing mortal hard. Mr. Sanderson?"

Silence.

"A pox on Mr. Sanderson," snapped Lady Margery. "Get me out of this directly or you'll hang at Tyburn for this night's work."

The servant went even whiter at the familiar note of authority in her voice. This was no doxy, as his master had led him to believe. Babbling apologies and pleas for forgiveness, he pulled her out of the carriage and lifted her down to the waiting arms of a groom who was standing in the ditch.

One carriage lamp was still miraculously burning, and in its flickering light Margery saw nothing but white desolation.

Villain or not, Toby must be saved. "Get your master out," she snapped. The small body of servants huddled round her. All appeared to be unhurt.

Margery turned her attention to the postilions. "Ride ahead and find the nearest inn and fetch help," she cried above the storm. "Tell them to prepare a bedchamber for your master and send someone to find a doctor."

The postilions relit their torches and rode off into the storm.

A faint groan was heard from the carriage. Margery stood numbly, with her torn cloak wrapped tightly about her, as Toby was dragged into view. He was very white and there was blood pouring down his face.

The servants pulled bearskin rugs out from the carriage and Margery wrapped herself in one, grateful for its shaggy warmth, and stood in the lee of the carriage. Toby's words seemed to be burned into her brain: "Said you was any man's for the asking."

Toby had collapsed once more into unconsciousness and Margery stared down at his prone form without pity. Perhaps she would feel sorry for him later, but now all she felt was a bitter hatred for this clumsy oaf who had mauled her and torn her clothes.

After what seemed an age, the storm abated a little and she could see the flickering light of the postilions' torches through the snow.

"Please, mum," said the first, pulling his forelock. "There's a posting inn, the George and Dragon, a ways down the road. The landlord's a surly cove and won't take out a carriage on a night like this for anybody. If you can ride, mum, you can take my 'orse and Jim and me" — he waved towards the other postilion — "will follow with the carriage horses and try to get Maister across the back o' one of 'em."

He dismounted from his horse as Margery nodded her head, and then threw her up into the saddle. The horse reared and curvetted, but she quickly brought it under control, glad there was no one else to see her but the servants as she galloped off astride the great beast, with her torn skirts hitched up above the knee.

It was only after a mile or so, when she saw the welcoming lights of the inn, that she realized it would have been better to have taken at least one servant with her, for appearance's sake. Tiny stinging pellets of snow whipped against her face and she realized with surprise that she was crying. She clumsily wiped the tears from her face with her sleeve and jumped down nimbly from the horse.

"Take this horse to the stables and rub it down," she called to the ostler, throwing him the reins.

The ostler grinned at her insolently, and she flushed with embarrassment as she realized her skirts were still hitched up. With frozen hands she tugged them back to a respectable length.

She turned her back on him and strode into the inn. It was expensively appointed and a cheerful fire crackled in the hall. She moved over to warm herself at it and then became aware that someone was staring at her. She swung round to face the landlord.

He was a fat, white man of immense girth, and with small piggy eyes, which were at the moment raking Margery up and down from her disheveled hair to the muddy wreck of her slippers.

Margery raised her eyebrows. "Arrange my room, sirrah!" she said coldly, "and then take yourself about your business."

The landlord fumbled in his waistcoat pocket and produced a goose quill and proceeded to clean his teeth in insolent silence.

"Speak, dog," said Margery, bristling like a small terrier.

"Ho, dog, is it?" said the landlord in a slow, plummy voice, "I'd rather be a dog than a doxy." He moved closer to her, grinning.

Margery's cloak fell open and a fine sapphire necklace, bought with her husband's generous allowance, blazed on her neck in the firelight.

The smile was wiped from the landlord's face. He paused, looking at the necklace as if hypnotized.

"And how dare you speak to me in those terms," said Margery. "I, sir, am the Marchioness of Edgecombe."

The smile was back on the landlord's face. "More like her ladyship's maid a-runnin' away with 'er jools," he said with a fat laugh.

A cold blast of wind heralded the arrival of another traveler. The landlord turned round, and immediately his fat face creased itself into obsequious smiles. He knew the quality when he saw it. The handsome, high-nosed stranger who was standing on the threshold was wearing a many-caped drab coat, gleaming Hessians, and a curly-brimmed beaver perched at a rakish angle on his thick tawny hair.

"And what," said Charles, Marquess of Edgecombe, "is my wife doing standing there unattended?"

The landlord goggled and a blush of dismay colored his face. "How was I to know?" he bleated. "How —"

"Cease your cackling, you fat whoreson," rapped the marquess. "A bedchamber for my lady and a private parlor. I also need accommodation for my friends."

Feeling faint and dizzy, Margery was aware that Amelia and Freddie had appeared behind the marquess. Amelia wrapped her motherly arms round her shivering niece.

"Come away, my dear," she said gently, as if talking to a hurt child. "There, my dear. There. Aunt Amelia is here and everything is going to be all right."

The marquess half reached out his hand to his wife as she left the room. But she shrank against Amelia and refused to look at him.

There was a further commotion in the doorway as Toby was carried in by the two ostlers. One of them recognized the marquess. "Maister will be all right, my lord," he said. " 'Tis only a blow to the head."

"Good," said the marquess grimly. "I am glad your master will live to give me the satisfaction I crave." Then he turned his back as Toby was carried abovestairs.

"Wasn't his fault," said Freddie as the marquess shrugged himself out of his coat. "It was yours."

The marquess's eyes narrowed. "Are you anxious to depart this world as well?" he asked in a deceptively mild voice.

"Pretty anxious," said Freddie gloomily. "Oh, stop looking daggers at me, Charles, and sit down. Hey, you! Landlord! Show us to that demned private parlor and bring the makings of a punch. I will need rum and arrack and . . . oh . . . cinnamon and lemons and hot water and cloves and —"

"I think that will do," remarked the marquess. "Go to it, man. Bustle about."

They followed the bowing and cringing landlord, who was still incoherently trying to apologize for his behavior to my lady, to the upper floor. The low-ceilinged parlor was cozy and warm, with thickly lined chintz curtains to keep out the winter drafts and a great fire roaring up the chimney. Both sat on either side of the fire in silence as the old inn rocked and heaved in the grasp of the storm and the landlord set the requisites for punch on a low deal table. Freddie rose and began to busy himself, sipping and tasting until he was satisfied. He then poured out two glasses and drained his own in one gulp. "May as well," he said half to himself, "since she won't have me."

"Won't have you," repeated the marquess wrathfully. "Are you another who has been attempting to seduce my wife?"

"Good God! No," said Freddie hurriedly. "I mean Amelia. Proposed, you know. But she won't have me."

"Then we share the same fate," said the marquess, kicking the logs with his boot.

"That's what I wanted to talk to you about," said Freddie cautiously. "But first of all, you know, you *did* tell Toby that any man could have your wife for the asking!"

The marquess went very white and still. "Then I cannot call Toby out," he said at last in an anguished whisper. "What an utter fool I've been, Freddie."

The door opened and Viscount Swanley strode in. He had been seeing to the rubbing down of the horses and was now prepared to relax. He was feeling justifiably proud of himself. Margery's reputation was saved. Toby would live and everyone would live happily ever after.

He stopped in dismay at the two grim faces in front of him. "What can be the matter?" he asked anxiously. "Were we not in time?"

"Oh, we were indeed in time. Everything is a garden of roses," said the marquess bitterly. "My wife has been told of my ill-judged remarks at Watier's and Amelia has refused Freddie. I have never known a woman to intrigue so much as Margery. She is probably sitting up in her room plotting some excellent way to get rid of me."

Margery was in fact pacing up and down her room like a small caged tiger, watched by her anxious aunt.

"Mayhap he was in his cups when he said those dreadful words," suggested Amelia hopefully.

"I shall never forgive him. Never!" said Margery passionately. "Living with Desdemona would be a better fate. But what of you, Amelia?"

Amelia blushed painfully. "Mr. Jamieson proposed marriage to me," she said in a whisper. "But I am too old for him. Perhaps now, if I told him that I had reconsidered, then I would be able to supply you with a home."

"Do you love him?" asked Margery bluntly.

For a few minutes there was no sound but the moan of the wind in the fireplace and the hissing whisper of snow against the panes.

"Yes," said Amelia softly. "But I am far too old. To tie a young man like that down —"

"Fiddle!" said Margery roundly. "Freddie is not nearly as stupid as he looks — sorry, Amelia — and had no doubt considered the matter carefully *and* has no doubt been ridiculed unmercifully by his so-good friends, Toby and Archie. But do not sacrifice yourself for me."

"If he loved me and if he knew what he was doing, then it would be no sacrifice," said Amelia slowly.

"Then forget about my agonies," said Margery brusquely. "Let one of us be happy. Go to him. Go immediately, Amelia. Throw yourself on his neck and tell him you love him. Please, my dear friend and aunt. You have done so much for me. Do this one thing for yourself. I shall contrive. I always have."

She smiled at her aunt's radiant face. Amelia looked very much younger than her years.

Trembling with fear and emotion, Amelia entered the private parlor and blinked at the light and at the three gentlemen seated there. Freddie, Perry, and the marquess rose to their feet and looked at her inquiringly. The marquess noticed with surprise that Amelia, with her eyes shining, her soft hair in a simple style under a demure lace cap, and her plump and shapely figure, still attired in a scarlet merino ball gown, was indeed a fine-looking woman.

"Servant, Lady Amelia," said the marquess, giving her his best bow. "Can we be of assistance to you?"

But Amelia had eyes for no one but Freddie.

Taking a deep breath, she said in a tremulous voice, "Mr. Jamieson. Earlier this evening you honored me with a proposal of marriage. I have decided to accept that proposal. Oh, F-Freddie, I am too old for you but I do love you so!"

Freddie had never been considered a man of action by his friends. But it seemed to take him two seconds to cross the parlor floor and clasp Amelia in his arms and kiss her passionately. The marquess felt a queer twist in his innards. Their love for each other was so powerful, it was practically tangible.

The emotional Perry had happy tears in his eyes. "Let's leave them alone," he whispered.

The marquess and Perry edged silently from the room, unnoticed by the happy couple. They paused outside the door. "Well, shall we descend to the tap?" asked Perry cheerfully.

The marquess slowly shook his head. "I am going to see my wife," he said slowly. "I feel I have wasted too much time already."

Lady Margery was turning over luxurious thoughts of vengeance in her mind. She would go to Desdemona and beg for a place. And Desdemona would humiliate her and treat her horribly, and *then* he would be sorry.

She would take a post as a governess and her employers would humiliate her and maybe beat her, and *then* he would be sorry.

But after a while her fantasies seemed as ridiculous as they in fact were. She must face the fact that her husband felt nothing for her. A tear rolled slowly down her cheek. There was a soft knock at the door and she brushed the tear angrily and went to answer it. Her husband stood on the threshold. She could not make out the expression on his face in the gloom, and shrank back.

He walked into the room and sat down in a low chair by the fire and stared into the flames. Margery slowly closed the door and came to stand over him, waiting for him to speak.

The marquess had been rehearsing many flowery and elegant speeches, but now he found that his throat was dry and that he was at a loss for words. Margery watched the firelight playing over his handsome face and elegant clothes as he sat back in the chair with one booted foot on the fender.

"The most damnable thing had happened," he said suddenly in his light husky voice without looking at her. "I have fallen in love with you and I don't know what to do about it.

"I was startled by the abandon of your lovemaking and mistook what I now realize was innocent passion for the art of an experienced woman."

Margery blinked in surprise.

"Perhaps you feel there is no hope for us. In that case I will release you and make provision for you so that you will not have to rely on Desdemona or your father."

She inched towards him, half frightened that he was playing some terrible joke.

"I was not in love with you when I married you. I knew I had to find a wife to produce an heir at some point. You were of good birth and in need of security. It seemed a fair bargain. I did not plan on falling in love you with, Margery. Rage and jealousy and possessiveness have made me unkind. I said terrible things about you at Watier's. Toby is a fool and not to be blamed for his actions.

"If you think that you could tolerate me, I would be happy with only that. I shall not press any intimate attentions on you."

There was a long silence while the marquess brooded sadly on the hopelessness of it all. With a start he realized Margery had whispered something.

"What!" he said, twisting round.

"I didn't fall in love with you when we were married," said Margery softly. "I had been in love with you for — oh, such a long time before that."

The marquess leaned back, limp with relief, in his chair and closed his eyes. With something like awe, she saw the glint of tears under his heavy lids and put her hand softly on his shoulder and bent her lips to his.

The marquess gave a groan and dragged her down onto his lap, kissing her and holding her and marveling at the miracle of recovering what he had so nearly lost.

Chapter Fourteen

The Earl of Chelmswood stood outside the windows of Rundell & Bridges with his countess clinging to his arm. He felt old and drained and tired. A bad run at the tables had sunk a great hole in the money he had received for Chelmswood, and now his countess was on the hunt for that necklace of Margery's. He dreaded the cost but even more did he dread his wife's temper.

"Come along," snapped Desdemona. "It is not in the window. You must ask inside."

It was a pale spring day with the first hint of warmth in the air. The earl thought longingly of Chelmswood as he had never done before. The daffodils would be out on the south lawn and the primroses in the hedgerows. He felt suddenly like a very elderly and very fallen angel, shut and barred from an English paradise.

With a little sigh, he entered the darkness of the shop, aware of his wife's predatory grasp on his arm.

Desdemona did not wait for him to speak. "That necklace," she cried to the first assistant, "— the diamond-and-ruby one which you had displayed in your window. I want it."

The assistant shook his head sadly. "You are too late, my lady. A gentleman bought it only the other day."

"Which gentleman?" hissed Desdemona.

"It was the Marquess of Edgecombe, my lady. He bought it for his wife."

"Fool!" screamed Desdemona, rounding on her husband. "This is what comes of your senile procrastination — you doddering *old man*."

Something seemed to snap in the earl's brain.

"I'll buy you a present, madam," he roared, happily oblivious of the staring eyes of the other customers. "You blood-sucking harpy. You can have a divorce as a present, that's what. You're nothing but a whited sepulcher — damme, if that ain't just it — a whited sepulcher, madam. All airs and graces on the outside, and inside, rotting with greed and spite and venom."

The countess looked at him in amazement. "But Jimmy . . ."

"Stow it!" said the earl rudely. "I'm going to sell that barracks in Grosvenor Square and I'm going to take the money and . . . and . . . damme, I'm going to buy Margery a demned wedding present instead of that cheap vase you insisted on. Here, fellow, bring out some of your best gems. Only the best for my daughter."

"I shall go back to mother," threatened Desdemona, as the earl's shaking hands began to turn over gem after gem.

"Bad cess to you, girl," said the earl, relishing his newfound armor of indifference. "Go find someone else."

Desdemona half ran from the shop, her eyes blurred with angry tears. He would pay and pay dearly for those insults. But as she stormed along the street, she began to think that it would be very difficult to revenge herself on a husband who held the purse strings.

"Hey, what's that? Beauty in distress, eh!"

Desdemona blinked the angry tears from her eyes and found herself looking into the mottled face of Colonel Andrew Chapman, a gambling crony of her husband.

"Oh, *Andy*," she burst out. "Jimmy is so horrid. He's going to *divorce* me!"

"Nonsense!" said the colonel. "Marriage spat, that's all."

"It's not a spat," wailed Desdemona, while her eyes neatly totaled up the cost of the colonel's expensive clothes to the last penny. "I — I shall run away with the first gentleman I meet —"

"Why! That's me!" exclaimed the colonel.

"The first gentleman who can take *care* of poor little Dessie properly," said Desdemona, casting a look up at the colonel from under her long lashes.

The colonel looked down at the beautiful face and exquisite form and his heart began to hammer like a drum. "Gawd, harrumph, ma'am. Should think any gentleman would be proud to . . . I declare, look at that fan in Asprey's. Cunning, ain't it? Little diamonds on the sticks, see. Just the sort of trifle a pretty gel like you should have, what!"

"Oh, I *couldn't*. I mean, I oughtn't," said Desdemona, nonetheless taking a little step towards the shop. "What would Jimmy say?"

"Don't matter anymore what Jimmy says," said the colonel, grandly offering his arm. "Just a little token of my esteem . . . the first, I hope, of many little tokens."

Desdemona gave him a blinding smile. "You have a wonderful way with words, my dear Colonel. A *wonderful* way with words . . ."

Toby Sanderson was tooling his curricle in the park at the fashionable hour. Lord Brenton was perched up beside him.

"There's Margery and Charles," said Archie. "Pull over and we'll join 'em."

Toby looked over to where the marquess's curricle was parked under the trees. The marquess and Margery were leaning down to talk to Amelia and Freddie. Four radiant faces on a perfect spring day. Margery said something and the marquess laughed and turned to kiss her on the cheek.

"They don't need us," said Toby sadly. "In fact, nobody does. We're just a pair of sour old bachelors."

He wheeled his team round and headed for the park gates.

"It's all your fault," said Archie. "You never listen to me. Didn't you see that pretty little Penelope Featherington at Almack's t'other Wednesday? The way she looked at you . . ."

"Miss Featherington is a very correct young lady," said Toby stiffly.

"Pooh!" said Archie rudely. "They all look like that on the outside, but get 'em between the sheets and they're all the same. Why, I could tell you a thing or two. I could —"

But whatever Archie could tell was destined never to be heard, by Toby at least.

Toby suddenly rammed his brother in the ribs with a beefy elbow and Archie somersaulted out of the curricle and landed heavily on the grass.

Toby whipped up his horses and bowled through the park gates at a smart pace. Quite suddenly, London looked like a jolly place again. He had not seen his old friends at the Four Horse Club for some time.

He would leave the petticoats alone and perhaps one day — just perhaps — he might land as lucky as Charles, Marquess of Edgecombe.

The employees of Thorndike Press hope you have enjoyed this Large Print book. All our Large Print titles are designed for easy reading, and all our books are made to last. Other Thorndike Press Large Print books are available at your library, through selected bookstores, or directly from us.

For information about titles, please call:

(800) 223-1244
(800) 223-6121

To share your comments, please write:

Publisher
Thorndike Press
295 Kennedy Memorial Drive
Waterville, ME   04901

DEMCO